THE LEGEND OF NIMWAY HALL: 1818 - ISABEL

SUZANNE ENOCH

The Legend of Nimway Hall: 1818 - Isabel

Copyright © 2018 by Suzanne Enoch

ISBN-13: 978-1985821163

ISBN-10: 1985821168

NYLA Publishing

350 7th Avenue, Suite 2003, NY 10001, New York.

http://www.nyliterary.com

❀ Created with Vellum

ABOUT THIS BOOK

1818: ISABEL

New York Times bestselling author Suzanne Enoch spins a Regency-era tale at Nimway Hall, in a book series centered on an estate where love and magic entwine to bring romance to all who dwell there.

A passionate, determined young lady trying to prove herself worthy of a magic-touched legacy, and a steadfast gentleman looking for his own place in the world join forces to restore an abandoned estate to its former glory.

The moment Isabel de Rossi turns eighteen, she takes charge of Nimway Hall, which has stood empty for the past ten years. Well-aware that all her female forebears found true love at Nimway, she can't wait to discover her own destined match. Instead she's faced with Adam Driscoll, the infuriatingly practical estate manager whose presence is a constant reminder that her own grandmother thinks she has no idea what she's doing.

Adam thought the recent offer of a position at Nimway Hall a godsend. After spending six years managing his elderly uncle's estate he is facing either a dreary career in the army or the church.

At Nimway his feet are on the ground, his hands in the earth, his mind on practical matters.

The last complication he needs is a foreign-raised heiress intent on finding a magical orb; but Adam can't help noticing that his strangely derailed repairs are suddenly on track, and that the clever, amusing mistress of the Hall is genuinely interested improving her estate and the lives of her tenants. And he is beginning to find it hard to resist his simmering attraction...

Isabel though wonders if she isn't worthy of becoming the property's guardian. The famous orb – the artifact reputedly responsible for every love match made at Nimway Hall is nowhere to be found...until dreamy Lord Alton arrives and starts to pursue Isabel. The pesky orb suddenly appears, though it seems to have a preference for the strong and loyal Adam.

For an unsophisticated young lady, the choice between a charming viscount and an interfering employee should be a simple one, but magic is a stubborn thing – and the heart is even more headstrong.

THE LEGEND OF NIMWAY HALL

A love invested with mystery and magic sends ripples through the ages.

Long ago in a cave obscured by the mists of time, Nimue, a powerful sorceress and Merlin's beloved, took the energy of their passion and wove it into a potent love spell. Intending the spell to honor their love and enshrine it in immortality, she merged the spell into the large moonstone in the headpiece of Merlin's staff. Thus, when Merlin was far from her, he still carried the aura of their love with him and, so they both believed, the moonstone would act as a catalyst for true love, inciting and encouraging love to blossom in the hearts of those frequently in the presence of the stone.

Sadly, neither Merlin nor Nimue, despite all their power, foresaw the heart of Lancelot. A minor adept, he sensed both the presence of the spell in the moonstone and also the spell's immense power. Driven by his own desires, Lancelot stole the headpiece and used the moonstone's power to sway Guinevere to his side.

Furious that the spell crafted from the pure love of his and his beloved's hearts had been misused, Merlin smote Lancelot and seized back the headpiece. To protect it forevermore, Merlin laid upon the stone a web of control that restricted its power. Henceforth, it could act only in response to a genuine need for true love, and only when that need impacted one of his and Nimue's blood, no matter howdistant.

Ultimately, Merlin sent the headpiece back to Nimue for safe keeping. As the Lady of the Lake, at that time, she lived in a cottage on an island surrounded by swiftly flowing streams, and it was in her power to see and watch over their now-dispersed offspring.

Time passed, and even those of near-immortality faded and vanished.

The land about Nimue's cottage drained, and the region eventually became known as Somerset.

Generations came and went, but crafted of spelled gold, the headpiece endured and continued to hold and protect the timeless moonstone imbued with Nimue's and Merlin's spells...

Over time, a house, crafted of sound local stone and timbers from the surrounding Balesboro Wood, was built on the site of Nimue's cottage. The house became known as Nimway Hall. From the first, the house remained in the hands and in the care of a female descendant of Nimue, on whom devolved the responsibilities of guardian of Nimway Hall. As decades and then centuries passed, the tradition was established that in each generation, the title of and responsibility for the house and associated estate passed to the eldest living and willing daughter of the previous female holder of the property, giving rise to the line of the Guardians of Nimway Hall.

THE GUARDIANS OF NIMWAY HALL
Nimue - Merlin.
through the mists of time

.

Moira Elizabeth O'Shannessy b. 1692

m. 1720 Phillip Tregarth

.

Jacqueline Vivienne Tregarth b. 1726
m. 1750 Lord Richard Devries

.

Olivia Heather Devries b. 1751
m. 1771 John "Jack" Harrington

.

Charlotte Anne Harrington b. 1776
m. 1794 Marco de Rossi

.

Isabel Jacqueline de Rossi b. 1797
m. 1818 Adam Driscoll

.

Miranda Rose Driscoll b. 1819
m. 1839 Michael Eades

.

Georgia Isabel Eades b. 1841
m. 1862 Frederick Hayden

.

Alexandra Edith Hayden b. 1864
m. 1888 Robert Curtis, Viscount Brynmore

.

Fredericka "Freddy" Viviane Curtis b. 1890
m. 1912 Anthony Marshall

.

Maddie Rose Devries b. 1904
m. 1926 Declan Maclean

.

Jocelyn Regina Stirling b. 1918
m.1940 Lt. Col. Gideon Fletcher

For my dad,
Who read every one of my books except this one.
I miss you.

CHAPTER 1

*N*one of the clocks at Harrington House in London seemed to be in working order. Isabel de Rossi had noted this oddity the moment she'd arrived in Town. As time passed – crawled by, really – she became convinced that every one of the clocks slowed even further. For the phenomenon to grow worse, the hands would have to begin moving backward.

"It's a clock, dear," her grandmother commented, stepping into the morning room. "You must have had clocks in Italy."

Isabel blinked, turning her gaze from the ornate gold mantel timepiece. "Hmm? Oh, of course we have clocks. I'm only... I'm eager to see Nimway Hall. I've heard about it all my life, after all."

"Nimway isn't going anywhere, I assure you." Grandmama Olivia gave a brief smile as she put an arm across Isabel's shoulders, guiding her granddaughter to the sofa. "Your grandfather and I haven't seen you since you were twelve, however, and I am selfish enough to wish to keep you here in London for more than three days. For heaven's sake, you've just turned eighteen, and you're in London. You should be anticipating a season of balls and dashing young men paying you compliments."

If she was being honest with herself, perhaps Isabel had

dreamed of that, from time to time. But having a Season meant an audience with royalty, doing perfect curtsies and knowing all the steps to every dance, and all the correct words to say to people with titles and gold-filigree names on their calling cards. Taking a deep breath, she suppressed a shudder. "I wasn't raised in anticipation of any of that," she offered.

"No, you were raised by Italians, for heaven's sake. Artistic Italians. I'm surprised you even wear clothes." She lifted an eyebrow. "You did wear clothes in Florence, didn't you?"

"Grandmama! Of course we wore clothes."

"Well, how am I to know? Your mother allowed herself to be sculpted nearly *nude* by your father, before they were even married. And all of his people were artists, he said."

"Yes, many of the de Rossis are sculptors. Quite celebrated ones." Olivia Harrington likely knew that already, but in Florence Isabel had grown up among some very talented sculptors, painters, musicians, and writers – even if none of those abilities had rubbed off on her. That didn't signify. Neither did she wish to mention that her father hadn't stopped at the Nimway Hall fireplace when it came to sculpting images of his wife Charlotte. And some of those had featured no clothing at all – including one displayed prominently on the landing of the main staircase at their home in Florence.

"I suppose someone must provide decorations for homes," her grandmother finally commented, with a smile that looked forced. "But my point is, you're not there now. You're here. And here, well-bred young ladies have Seasons."

"I don't wish for one. I've been looking after the household in Italy practically since I was twelve, Grandmama. I am ready for this. Isn't that why you wrote me that it was time I take over responsibility for Nimway Hall? Mama already gave me papers signing her ownership rights over to me. Was it all only a ruse to lure me here? Because I—"

"Of course it wasn't a ruse. I only hoped you would be more... reasonable than your mother." She flipped a hand at the air as if batting away an insect – or some past annoyance. "I have learned my lesson, however. Whatever I might have wished for Charlotte, and whatever I might wish for you, I will satisfy myself with supporting whichever path you choose for yourself." For a moment she looked not quite sad, but thoughtful. "I pushed your mother too hard, and so I can only blame myself for losing her to that Marco de Rossi and his gypsy Italians." Olivia looked up again. "But I don't wish to have to wait another twelve years to see you again. If you consider that a ruse, then I suppose I'm guilty."

Isabel was fairly certain no de Rossi had ever been a gypsy, but at the same time, her upbringing at the hands of her over-indulgent mother and her adoring father did seem a deliberate counterpoint to Olivia and Jack Harrington's much stricter views. Somewhere in the middle would have been nice – and considerably more useful, really. "Somerset isn't so very far from London. It's much closer than Florence, certainly."

Grandmama Olivia smiled again. "It is much closer, yes." The older woman reached beyond Isabel to pick up an embroidery hoop. She gave it a perfunctory glance and set it on Isabel's lap. "I'm not one to criticize, but I believe even Miss Tatterbell could improve on this rose."

Isabel sighed, sending an annoyed glance at the tabby cat in the front window. "It's supposed to be a strawberry."

"Ah." Olivia rang the small bell on the side table, and a moment later a footman appeared in the doorway. "Tea if you please, Tom."

"Yes, ma'am."

Biting her tongue against the wish to point out that she hadn't journeyed all the way from Florence, Italy, to London, England, to embroider, Isabel poked the needle several times through the fabric. She *had* missed seeing her grandparents, and being in London *was* rather exciting. But she didn't need anyone else to tell her that she wasn't meant for proper Society, for soirees or evenings at the theater. For eighteen years she'd heard tales of Nimway Hall and its mysteries, and she wanted to see them for herself. The sooner, the better.

Sighing, she dropped the embroidery hoop back onto her lap. "Grandmama, if you've changed your mind, or if you think I'm not...capable of taking over the care of Nimway, I wish you would simply say so." It would be painful, but at least she would know. At least she would be able to stop waiting for...something. For this restlessness that had begun a year or so ago to stop pushing at her.

"If I hadn't thought you ready, I wouldn't have written you and your mother about it." Olivia nodded her thanks as tea appeared. "Shut the door, Tom," she instructed, and the footman did so. "And I know how little Charlotte cares for household duties and that you've been seeing to them on your mother's behalf. However, that said, your grandfather's leg is likely to heal within a few weeks, and we could return to Nimway Hall with you. All see it together, as it were."

"Grandpapa Jack shouldn't be fox hunting at his age," Isabel returned, accepting the cup of tea her grandmother poured then adding three lumps of sugar and a splash of milk to the watery concoction. The secret to drinking tea, she'd discovered, was to make certain it didn't taste like itself.

"You are not the first one to say so," Olivia commented, sitting back in her seat and sipping.

"But his leg is not the reason you've been gone from the estate for ten years. His leg being healed is therefore not the reason you would wish to make a return to it."

Her grandmother eyed her over the rim on her porcelain cup, which was trimmed with silver and featured a flock of blue doves circling some sort of shrubbery. "You're a clever thing, aren't you?"

"I do try to be."

"Cleverness isn't always a welcome trait, especially when one is seeking a husband."

Isabel blinked. "I'm not seeking a husband. I'm seeking a chance to become Nimway Hall's guardian, just as you did. And as Mother did not."

"She did, in her way. As long as her heart continues to beat, my

Charlotte protects the land and our people. As do I. As will you. Nimway can be a large and demanding mistress, Isabel. And a duty not lightly taken, nor lightly set aside." She sat forward again, lowering the cup and her voice. "And as you are the only daughter, the only child, of your generation, you will also be required to produce an heir. Which means that yes, you are seeking a husband. The female line must continue."

Well, she hadn't thought of it that way. After eighteen years in Italy, broken by a holiday or two to England, she'd wanted to come home. And though she couldn't explain it, and though she'd never even set eyes on it, Nimway Hall was home. Not the large, rambling house in Florence or her loving, contented parents, or the loud, boisterous extended Italian family on her father's side and the conclave of artists that had always surrounded them. Yes, she loved them all, and she missed them dearly, but for nearly all her life something had pulled at her. She needed to go home.

Olivia patted her on the knee, making her jump. "Nimway Hall will affect you," she said, her voice soft and her gaze unfocused, as if she'd become lost in a daydream. "It's a busybody and has no qualms about pushing people into directions they would not choose to go if left to their own devices." She shook herself a little, her gaze returning to her granddaughter. "You know your grand-father and I did not favor a match between Charlotte and Marco de Rossi. An artist – a sculptor, for heaven's sake – and an Italian. He dared carve your mother's half-clothed image on our dining room fireplace." She shuddered, nearly spilling her tea. "I can assure you, that is nothing a mother or a father wants to see on a daily basis."

"But Papa is a master sculptor," Isabel couldn't help retorting.

"Yes, he is, which means no one could mistake the identity of his subject, bared to the view of every diner from now to eternity." She set her tea aside. "But the Hall thought nothing of that. I think it likes strong feelings, and...lustful thoughts, and all manner of unacceptable behaviors."

"You...talk about Nimway likes it's alive," Isabel commented.

Her mother seemed to believe so, but Grandmama Olivia was so much more practical than her daughter Charlotte. "Surely—"

"Yes, you may think I'm a madwoman. I did as well, when we lived there." Olivia stood, then walked to the writing desk and pulled a large, leather-bound stack of papers from a drawer. "And *that* is why I intend to remain in London and why I agreed to pass it on to you now. I still urge you to stay on with us here, my darling, at least until you can be assured that you won't have to walk through the front door alone."

"I won't be alone. I'll have Jane with me."

"Your companion is not a protector. Not unless she can wield a musket." Frowning, Olivia reached down for Isabel's tea and set it aside as well, then took her granddaughter's hands and turned them palm up. "And no, I don't think you'll require a musket. I'm merely… I'm getting to be an old woman, so don't mind what I say. Only do be cautious. As I said, the house affects everyone differently. You may not like what it does to you. But for better or worse, it's now yours."

With that, she set the papers onto Isabel's palms. They felt heavy, but then keeping a house within the female line of a family had taken a considerable amount of paperwork through the years. A rush of excitement swept up her spine as she clutched the bundle to her chest. A house, a mansion, abandoned for ten years and all hers. Hers, to shape and guide, to put her own stamp upon. And the magic of Nimway Hall, the mysterious orb and the bountiful crops and the ancient Balesboro Wood that confused foes and aided friends, the place of wizards and ladies of the lake, knights in shining armor – it belonged to her now. Finally.

"I should tell you," her grandmother went on, releasing her hand and turning for the morning room doorway, "when I decided to write you, I had our solicitor hire a new steward for Nimway Hall. I would have preferred to leave you with Prentiss in charge, but now I'm discovering that he may have become a bit eccentric in his later years, and a property as large as Nimway

Hall certainly can't manage without a steward. No sense in you arriving to see a tumbled ruin or overgrown garden."

Oh. A steward. Of course there would be one, but for heaven's sake, her grandmother might have waited another month or two and let the new guardian of Nimway hire her own. How could it be her home if someone else, some random man hired by random men, had barged in before she could ever arrive? A man who would no doubt have a criticism for everything she attempted and who'd probably already seen to everything she'd wanted to do herself. "Do I have to keep him on?"

"The steward? Of course not. But Mr. ... what was it? Ripple? Dripple? At any rate, he presently knows more about Nimway Hall than you do. And if we – I, at least – go about hiring and sacking employees willy-nilly, people will think us frivolous. Will think *me* frivolous. So please keep that in mind."

"Will he answer to you, or to me?"

"Well, you, of course. Though I did hire him. Just listen to his suggestions and keep my reputation in mind before you sack him and hire someone else. I don't doubt your enthusiasm, but you've run a household – not an estate. There is a difference. Believe me. Now. You will be staying for luncheon and dinner, I hope? Or are you in such a hurry to leave that you don't even have a moment for goodbyes?"

Isabel set aside the bundle of papers and stood to hurry over to wrap her arms around her grandmother's slender waist. "I am never in that much of a hurry, and I never will be. I know you have your doubts, but I don't."

Olivia put a finger beneath her granddaughter's chin and kissed her forehead. "And that is why I'm worried."

CHAPTER 2

"*P*atience is a virtue," Adam Driscoll recited under his breath, the fiftieth time he'd done so since awakening that morning. It had begun with his left boot going missing, and hadn't improved since then. Nodding at the barrel of a man behind him, he wrapped the heavy rope around his leather-gloved hands. "Ready? One, two, three, pull!"

Slowly, groaning and reluctant, the millstone in front of them left its partner and lifted an inch or two into the air. With each coordinated heave on the rope, it rose another fraction. The old thing weighed close to two tons, but the mill helped the valley prosper. It needed to be repaired, and thankfully the farmers who lived on the Nimway Hall property knew that.

"I need at least a foot, or I won't be able to reach in to grind off that ridge," the stonemason they'd brought in from Glastonbury grunted, putting his fingers over the lip – which seemed a highly unwise thing to do given the path the four weeks of Adam's stewardship had taken.

"Mr. Reynolds," Adam panted, planting his recovered boot – which had thankfully been located behind the wardrobe, of all things – against the straw-covered stone floor and taking in another inch of rope, "I do not recommend—"

The wooden crossbeam snapped in two. Even as the thunderous sound registered, the rope went slack in his hands. Adam went over backward, falling hard on the quartet of farmers behind him. Before he could even pull breath back into his lungs, he forced himself to his feet, expecting to see the stonemason's hand crushed between the two massive burrstone slabs.

Instead, the ten-fingered Tom Reynolds crouched down, picked up a piece of discarded straw, and stuck it between his teeth. "You need a sturdier pulley rig, I reckon," he observed.

Adam brushed straw from his backside and tried not to cough as the mill dust rose and twirled around them. They'd bound together three eight-inch-thick tree trunks. The cross beam should have been sturdy enough to lift the entire mill, much less the runner stone. He'd assisted; the rig had been well made. The other men, including Phillip Miller, the aptly-named miller, had begun cursing and making signs against the evil eye. And they were sending sideways glances at him again.

As much as he wanted to proclaim his innocence in the fiasco, Adam had begun to realize over the past four weeks he'd resided at Nimway Hall that they didn't doubt his competence. They doubted his presence, and his luck. And there wasn't much he could do about that except to persist. This property was worth it. The position he'd found for himself was worth it.

He made his way through the flour dust and the wreck of the pulley system to crouch beside the crossbeam. They'd used fresh-cut timber because it would be more likely to flex and bend than break. He would have been tempted to call it deliberate, except he could see absolutely no sign of a saw or blade mark.

"Will you be putting me up tonight, then?" the stonemason asked, leaning over him.

Adam straightened. For the first time the muscular-armed mason's aloof expression faded, and he took a half- then a full-step back. "Patience is a virtue," Adam repeated to himself, and straightened his fingers. "Yes, Mr. Reynolds. I'll have a room waiting for you at the Two-Headed Dragon. I've been told it's the finest inn in Balesborough."

"I reckon that'll do for me, Mr. Driscoll. Thank you." He narrowed one eye as he continued to chew on the straw sticking out from between his teeth. "That was a fine contraption. It should have worked," he offered after a moment.

Yes, it should have. And the plan to smoke the bees out of the attic should have worked, but that had only gotten him stung three times and sent the creatures into two of the servants' rooms as well as the large storage room up there. He could hear them humming above his head in the evenings. Re-setting the iron railing that bordered the back terrace should also have been a simple task, but a freak rainstorm had poured so much water into the concrete mix that it wouldn't set. That hadn't been his fault, except that as the property's steward, he evidently should have known better than to make the attempt.

"The Hall won't like you poking about," Simmons the butler had informed him. His reply that the Hall would like being readied for its owner's return had been met with an even more concise, "No, it won't." Evidently, either the butler had precognitive abilities, or his unending dour predictions occasionally bore fruit.

Stripping off his gloves and noting another blister on his left palm, Adam sent the miller and two others to find more suitable logs for another attempt in the morning. The farmers seemed perfectly content to return tomorrow, but then Adam had the sneaking suspicion that they anticipated seeing what might go wrong next more than they did seeing the millstone repaired. After all, the harvest wouldn't be ready for another month or two, at best. They had time to be amused.

Outside, he shook more grain dust out of his hair and collected his mount. With a cluck, he sent the big chestnut gelding east in the direction of the steep escarpment and Nimway Hall above.

Off to his right, Miller the miller guided two heavy plow horses more southerly toward Balesboro Wood for the additional lumber they would need tomorrow. All of the farmers and other residents on the substantial acreage owned by Mrs. Olivia Harrington had been friendly and cooperative, if doubtful of his success. They acknowledged that some upkeep and repairs were needed, and they'd been swift to offer assistance – and opinions, of course.

None of them – and he considered himself a fair judge of character – struck him as being duplicitous or underhanded. The accidents and misfortunes presently thwarting him didn't seem to be either malicious or intentional. In a sense, though, his inability to explain any of it left him even more frustrated. None of this lay beyond his experience or his abilities; in fact, as he'd made his initial assessment of the estate after his arrival, he'd thought bringing it back to its former glory would be simple.

The Harringtons had only been away for ten years, and the house had maintained a reduced staff for that time. The former steward, Mr. Prentiss, had apparently decided that challenging the house would be unwise, but money had clearly gone toward general maintenance as well as toward keeping up the mill, the community vegetable garden, and the irrigation systems, and the farms had prospered even without their landlord's presence. And yet.

He let the chestnut set its own pace, and they ascended the narrow, twisting trail up the face of the escarpments at a walk. He'd seen carts navigate the path, but he would hate to have to do it at night or in bad weather.

Nimway had both long history and care showing in every beam and cornice, along with a warmth that reminded him of his own home. But here, all that history kept eyeing him, unsettling him whenever he even considered making repairs. Strictly speaking he was an intruder, but at least he was an invited one. And he had nothing but admiration for what he saw around him.

He could always uninvite himself, but he refused to give up

after only four weeks. He was a fourth son; fighting for things had become nearly second nature. And employment like this, at a place like this, wasn't likely to come along again any time soon, if ever. And certainly not for a man of five-and-twenty.

At eighteen, just as he'd decided that, as the fourth son of a minor baron, he had what amounted to a choice between the priesthood and the army – which meant choosing the army – his uncle had turned over a carriage and broken one leg beyond healing. The physician had removed it above the knee. For the subsequent seven years, Adam had served as the Franklin Park steward, its guardian, and the confidante of his seven younger female cousins. Just six months ago, Margaret, the oldest cousin, had come of age and found a husband who thankfully had been competent enough that just in the past fortnight he'd taken over the steward position.

Adam sent the chestnut along the southernmost pathway, the one that bordered the edge of Balesboro Wood. It would add an additional thirty minutes or so to reach Nimway Hall by this route, but he needed those moments to figure out where they'd erred with the pulley so it wouldn't happen again. Purple and red splashed the western sky behind him, and a trio of does stepped into the meadow then retreated again when they caught sight of him.

He'd enjoyed directing Franklin Park in a way he'd never expected. Given his circumstances, however, owning acreage of his own seemed supremely unlikely. He'd therefore thought it fortuitous that just as he'd found himself replaced at Franklin, the solicitor father of an old friend had written to inquire if he was available to take up a newly-vacated position at Nimway Hall.

Adam had barely paused long enough to pack a trunk. Now, however, he wasn't so certain that "fortuitous" had been the correct word. In fact, despite his determination to succeed at *something* here, over the past few days he'd begun to wonder if resigning might be in the best interests of everyone involved. Tom Reynolds might have been badly injured today.

He shook himself. Coincidence. The offer of employment – a coincidence. A stewardship position coming available also happened to be very rare. A steward tended to serve until he was too old to do so, at which time a son would assume the position. It was almost a commoner's version of a title inheritance. The one at Nimway Hall had been unusual both in the fact that the previous steward had conveniently expired in the village's cemetery, and that he had no sons and hadn't suggested anyone else to succeed him. Adam knew he wasn't likely to run across another such opportunity.

And if the circumstances of his employment were coincidence, then so were the misfortunes that had plagued him since his arrival. The nonsense wasn't anything he'd done, and it therefore had no reason to continue. All it would take was a bit more determination. And he had that in spades.

Just how long he might have remained pondering his future while the sky darkened around him he didn't know, because as the path joined with the road that wound from the manor house and back through the wood, something caught his attention.

A lone owl hooted, and he shook himself back to the present. He'd best turn back to the manor before the staff could think he'd fled – giving him something else to explain. A second owl joined the first, then a third, and a fourth.

Adam pulled up the gelding. In a moment the entire wood reverberated with "Hoo-hoo". The hairs on his neck lifted. What in the world would upset every owl in Somerset? A fire? He narrowed his eyes scanning the edge of the forest, but no light caught his eyes. He didn't smell smoke, though the sky was too dark now for him to see it.

His mount sidestepped, chuffing nervously. Tightening his hand on the reins, Adam reached down his free hand to pat the beast on the neck. "Easy now, boy."

Then, light did catch his gaze. Firelight, but contained, floating and blinking, drifted toward him. Two lights, then four, bobbing as they approached. The owls stopped. The wood seemed to hold its breath, silent and still and waiting. No crickets, no frogs, broke the silence.

As he watched the lights moving closer, a light breeze touched his face. In the same moment, a pair of crickets began chirping off to his left, and he realized what the lights must be. Carriage lamps. A coach, approaching through Balesboro Woods.

Of course it was a coach. What the devil else would it be? Blowing out his breath, he kneed the gelding off the worn road as the vehicle emerged from the wood. "Nimway Hall?" the black-clothed driver asked as they drew even.

"Follow this road, about half a mile on," Adam responded. "Who comes?"

"The Hall's mistress."

Olivia Harrington? Adam wheeled the gelding to follow the coach. Behind him, a lone owl hooted once more. He slowed, listening, but the sound echoed into silence without being repeated. The disturbance, whatever had unsettled the birds of prey, seemed to have ceased. Nevertheless, he kept glancing over his shoulder all the way back to the well-lit hall.

As the coach stopped before the front portico Adam dismounted, handing the reins to Toby as the lad ran up from the stables at the rear of the house. The boy gawped, wide-eyed, as the coach driver flipped down the steps and the plain black door swung open.

At the same moment the ancient butler, Simmons, appeared from somewhere to hold out his hand. Adam had known the man for a month and had never seen him move that quickly. A yellow-gloved hand reached out from the coach's cavernous darkness, fingers curling around the butler's. Then a foot, sheathed in a dainty yellow walking slipper, emerged, followed by a yellow and green muslin walking dress patterned with tiny red flowers, then a massive yellow bonnet that obscured everything above the woman's shoulders.

Both feet touched the ground, and Adam stepped forward. "Mrs. Harrington? I wasn't expecting you. I'm—"

She lifted her head, and the words stopped in his throat. As far as he knew, Olivia Harrington was a grandmother, a woman of at least middle age. The deep-gray eyes looking up at him didn't belong to a grandmother. And neither did the deep brown curls of burnished mahogany that framed her temples. "Mrs. Harrington is my grandmother," she said, in well-educated tones, her accent touched by something he couldn't quite put a name to. "I am Isabel de Rossi. And you would be Mr. Dingle?"

"Driscoll," he corrected. Evidently neither of them had expected the other. "Adam Driscoll."

"Ah, yes. Driscoll." She sent her gaze down to his boots and back up again.

Abruptly he realized the sight he must look. "I must apologize," he said, brushing at his coat. "As I said, I wasn't expecting anyone." He cleared his throat. "Simmons, she'll be wanting the master bedchamber. And inform Mrs. Dall we'll have two more for dinner."

"Miss de Rossi," Simmons intoned, bowing and nearly knocking Adam aside. "I knew your mother well. How fares Miss Charlotte?"

Isabel smiled, thankful for all the tales her mother used to tell of Nimway Hall and its residents, and for the moment to think about something other than the annoying man who was already giving orders on her behalf when she could speak quite well for herself. "Simmons. My mother speaks of you often. She and my father are both quite well, thank you."

The butler's cheeks colored beneath his shock of white hair. "I'm honored that she remembers me. A fine young lady, she was." With a blink he snapped back to attention. "Will, see that the mistress's things are brought up to the master bedchamber. And have the room opened. We cannot have her sleeping on furniture coverings and dust."

A younger man, one of the footmen, she presumed, flashed by to begin untying her substantial luggage from the rear of the coach. Behind her Jane stepped down to the ground as well. "We might have stopped for the night in East Pennard or Balesborough," Isabel commented, reminding herself that this moment would serve as the servants' first impression of her, "but I was very eager to reach the Hall. And I don't mind a bit of dust."

And as badly as she wanted to gaze up at the building, to run inside and explore and find...something that could explain the breathless excitement she felt, the reason she'd decided they would drive all night if necessary to reach Nimway Hall without another stop, she couldn't very well behave like a flighty girl. She was the mistress of this property now.

The rather tall Mr. Driscoll continued to stand between her and the front door. She didn't know precisely whom she'd expected, but certainly not someone as...fit as he appeared. She'd met a steward or two, and they'd been older, experienced men, selected for their ability to maintain the running of an estate while its master was elsewhere. They served as the owner's surrogate. They didn't have straw sticking up from their dark, disheveled hair or patches of dust on their sleeves. For heaven's sake, he looked more like a farmer than a steward.

A handsome farmer, to be sure, black haired and green eyed with a lean hardness to his body and his face. A man who worked with his hands, from the look of his attire, and one who no doubt thought he knew everything about Nimway Hall and how best to run it. Well, she would see about that. She might not know precisely what Nimway needed – yet – but she would figure it out. Because this was where she belonged.

Isabel took a deep breath and stepped around Adam Driscoll. Tonight, she wanted to see Nimway Hall. She could sack the steward tomorrow.

CHAPTER 3

"What do you think, Jane?" Isabel asked, kneeling in front of the alabaster figure carved into the left side of the large white-marble fireplace. The formal dining room had, of course, been her first stop on her tour.

"It's... Good heavens."

"It's exquisite." She recognized her mother in every line of Marco de Rossi's work, even though twenty years in age lay between the sculpture and the woman she'd last seen a month ago. The carving and Charlotte Harrington-de Rossi were twins, one idealized and young forever while the other had become a wife and a mother.

"You shouldn't be looking at it, Isabel. It's..." Jane lowered her voice to a whisper. "It's naked."

"Only partly." And it truly didn't bother her. Perhaps that was because naked art and Florence couldn't exist without each other, or perhaps it was because this was how her father had viewed her mother when the two of them were just falling in love. A magic moment, captured forever.

And that was why the dining room had been her first destination once she stepped through the front door of Nimway Hall.

She studied the white marble for another ten minutes, understanding why it made her grandparents uncomfortable – though she suspected that their…dismay had had at least as much to do with the realization that Charlotte wouldn't be living the life they'd envisioned for her as it did with seeing an idealized breast in white marble.

As for Isabel, she found the carving comforting. Her parents were here even if they remained an ocean away. The statue's nudity didn't bother her, because she felt it more than she saw it, felt the warmth and love and life in the hands that had made it and the way he'd seen – and still saw – the woman whose image he'd sculpted.

When Jane's chest crossing and hand wringing became too much to ignore, Isabel stood again. "Shall we see the rest of the house, then? I want to find that orb Mama always talked about." She said it as casually as she could, but a magic orb seemed both impossible and inevitable, and she wanted – needed – to set her eyes on it. The sooner, the better.

"Oh, thank heavens. Can you imagine perfect strangers seeing that fireplace? Or worse yet, acquaintances? Mr. Driscoll has seen it, certainly. Mortifying!"

Once more biting back her reply, Isabel nodded as she made her way down to the library. Like the rest of Nimway Hall thus far it stood elegant and tasteful and feeling not old, but…ancient. No, not ancient, either. Timeless, more like. As though it had always been there and always would be. Guardians could add to the collection or re-organize the shelves, but this was where their centuries of stories slept.

She took a deep breath. "I think I shall spend a great deal of time here."

"I imagine there are enough books about Merlin and knights and dragons here to satisfy even you," Jane agreed, walking over to run a finger along the shelves, then stifled a yawn. "I know you wish to see everything, but we've been traveling since dawn."

That, they had been. And Jane was seventeen years her senior

– certainly not old, but probably less…enchanted at finally being here than she was. Seeing the remainder of the house while she was awake enough to appreciate it. She had the rest of her life to explore, after all. This was now home. "We'll begin again in the morning, shall we?" she said, and took Jane's arm.

"Oh, yes, please. I'm near to falling asleep standing up."

Jane had taken the next room down from hers, and Isabel sent her off to bed before she put on her own night rail. That done, she had one more thing she needed to do before she went to bed. Beginning with the bookshelf and working her way around the room, she shifted every book, every knick-knack, every chair, every potted plant, and every candle. After hearing so many tales about the orb, she half-expected it to fly into the room and land on the bed. Dash it all, it wasn't here, though. Isabel took a last look about, then blew out the lamp by her bed. She had a great many more places to look, and however eager she might be, tomorrow would have to be soon enough.

Finally she sank beneath the warm sheets in the master bedchamber. She spent the night dreaming about swords emerging from lakes, a bearded man with an ornate staff and holding a young girl by the hand, and a pair of deep-green eyes.

When she opened her own eyes in the morning, it took a moment before she remembered where she was. Isabel sat up and stretched.

The Nimway Hall master bedchamber took up the entire end of the west wing, with windows overlooking the woods to the south, Myrrden Lake to the north beyond the gardens, and to the northwest a view of the ancient Tor at Glastonbury.

She'd known all that before she arrived, though. After years of pestering her mother for every ounce of information about their ancestral home, years spent devouring books about Somerset and especially Glastonbury – after all, Arthur and Guinevere were rumored to be buried at the ruined cathedral there – she doubted there could be anything she *didn't* know about the layout and history of Nimway Hall.

Except for the name of the steward, of course. Isabel frowned as she untangled herself from the bedsheets and stood. That had been stupid of her. She knew his name to be Adam Driscoll, and at the last moment she'd selected one of her grandmother's misnomers to address him. No, she didn't need him, and she'd been attempting to illustrate that fact, but it had felt needlessly unkind.

"Never mind that now," she muttered, pushing hair out of her eyes. Who hired such a young man to oversee as large and ancient an estate as Nimway Hall, anyway? Stewards were stooped-over old men with ink stains on their fingers. Oh, wait, perhaps she was thinking of solicitors or clerks. Anyway, they didn't have straw in their hair or on their jackets, and they didn't have keen and curious green eyes or tower over her as if being three inches over five feet made her a midget.

Surely her grandmother hadn't known her solicitors were hiring such a young man for the position. At best she'd hoped for a kindly old man to introduce her about. At worst – well, she hadn't imagined a worst, but a towering, energetic young man who thought he knew everything about Nimway Hall – that would be it.

"Oh, stop it, Isabel," she told herself, as she walked to the southern-facing set of windows and tugged the curtains open. It was done, and now for her own peace of mind she would have to demonstrate that she wasn't some nodcock before she sent Adam Driscoll packing, even if it was purely her own pride speaking. Taking a slow breath, she lifted her eyes to the view outside the window.

Beyond a large meadow and a picturesque scattering of white sheep, the woods loomed thick and dark, visible all the way to the drop-off to the west, and curving up and around to the east. Mist hung in the tops of the trees, beginning to sparkle as the rising sun touched it. Rainbows darted here and there, appearing and immediately vanishing in the rapidly altering light. She'd never seen such colors. There couldn't possibly be words invented to describe all the hues.

She watched the spectacle, mesmerized, until the sun inched high enough to strike the scene directly and return the display to simple mist and trees again. Did such a thing happen every sunrise? Had it been especially for her?

Perhaps only a child should ask such a question. But then she'd known since her childhood that Nimway Hall *was* magical. Her mother, Charlotte, had said so many times, even if she'd pretended to explain some of the occurrences away as Isabel had gotten older. Even if the same bedtime stories had gone from being true events to fairy tales. Isabel knew which version she believed.

Strict Grandmama Olivia had as much as said the house was alive, and if there was ever a more skeptical person than Olivia Harrington, Isabel had never met her. Or him.

Leaving the south-facing curtains open, she wandered to the other end of the huge room, running her fingers along chair backs and up the bedposts as she did so. They – her parents – had a lovely home in Florence, and her papa could trace some of the furniture pieces there all the way back to the Italian Renaissance. But that had been his side of the family, the one she'd always thought of as the male side. This, Nimway Hall, felt like the female side, and she didn't think that was entirely because it passed to the eldest daughter in the female line. The house itself felt...motherly, warm, welcoming, and accepting. Or perhaps she was imagining it because she so badly wanted it t—

"Get out of there, Driscoll! You'll be killed!"

Heavens! Isabel stepped into her coach slippers and threw on a heavy dressing robe, then flung open her door and hurried for the nearest third-floor stairs. Just beyond the small attic hallway a half dozen servants milled, several of them missing jackets and one with no shoes. A distinct humming sound filled the air as she approached. The butler, Simmons, held closed the door she thought opened into the upstairs storage room, his ear pressed hard against it.

"What is going on?" she demanded, as the muffled humming grew louder.

The butler started. "I beg your pardon, Miss Isabel. I – You—" He paled, waving his hands in front of the trio of male servants present. "Avert your eyes! Miss Isabel, you – you're naked."

Frowning, she glanced down at herself. A night rail, a heavy dressing gown over that, and house slippers, which were more layers than she wore when she had a proper dress on. *Englishmen.* "I'm not naked, for goodness' sake. Now why were you shouting?"

He scowled. "But you—"

"Simmons, I dress as I please. Where is Mr. Driscoll?" She asked the question crisply, and the butler visibly shook himself.

"Ah. Yes. If nudity is acceptable these days, then so be it. That daft Driscoll's gone in to smoke out the bees. The last time we tried it, half of us were nearly stung to death, but now he's in there alone."

"We have bees in the attic?" she asked, feeling a bit as if she'd opened a book somewhere in the middle, without knowing the characters or the plot. Her fairy tales had never featured bees. Her real life featured bees.

"Yes, ma'am. For the past three weeks. We've lost four rooms up here to them now."

Surreptitiously tucking her hands up into the thick, puffy sleeves of the dressing gown and glad she'd buttoned it to her chin, Isabel padded up to the door in her house slippers. "I would like to see what's happening, if you please."

"But Miss Isa—"

"Crack open the door so I can see. In fact, step back. I'll see to it. If Mr. Driscoll is injured we'll need to figure a way to get him out of there." She motioned the other servants to back away as a precaution. Then, leaning against the doorframe, she put her robe-covered hand over the handle and pushed down. The latch lowered, and the door opened a fraction. Buzzing sounds filled the air. Definitely honey bees. She lifted her shoulders to help protect her neck and widened the opening.

The sight inside froze her for a moment. Bees swirled through a haze of pleasant-smelling smoke, their attention on the figure standing in the middle of the room. He wore heavy work gloves, one of them holding the smoker. Mr. Driscoll also wore a very large woman's hat, a heavy lace sewn all around the wide brim and hanging down past his shoulders. It looked as though he'd donned at least half a dozen progressively-larger jackets, and she would have been ready to swear that he also had on multiple pairs of trousers, all stuffed into an overlarge pair of stable boots.

All the windows beyond him stood open, but the bees didn't show any sign of flying away. Rather, they swarmed around the large dresser in front of him as he flipped it sideways in the direction of the nearest window. Bees frantically flew in and out from the turned-over bottom of the piece and over the front of the veil. She realized immediately that he couldn't use the smoker and move the dresser at the same time.

Swiftly she grabbed up the second smoker that stood just inside the doorway, turned it on herself in hopes the bees would ignore her, then moved into the room. "I'll smoke them," she said, pumping the top to send streams of smoke around her and suppressing a cough. "You move the dresser."

"Miss de Rossi!" he exclaimed from beneath the heavy curtain of lace. "You cannot—"

"I *am*," she interrupted, puffing smoke in his direction. "No delays, now."

As she approached him, sliding her slippered feet along the floor to avoid stepping on any smoke-downed bees, the humming began to lower in pitch, sounding less frantic and angry. The additional smoker must have helped, because the swirling swarm slowed, closing in around their chosen piece of furniture, and thinned as the bees returned to their hive somewhere inside the heavy mahogany dresser.

The dresser Mr. Driscoll meant to heave out a third-floor

window. "Wait," she breathed, as he crouched over the dresser. "Could you wrap it in blankets?"

The lady's hat swiveled from her to the multitude of pieces of covered furniture around them. "Keep smoking the dresser," he instructed. He slowly and quietly stepped around to her side and removed his hat. Before she could object, he placed it over her head, carefully adjusting the hanging lace around her so it hung down around her shoulders. "I won't have you getting stung," he commented.

It was thoughtful, considering that he still faced the bee horde, himself. Still easing his way through the smoke and settling bees, he squinted his eyes against the thickening smoke and stripped blankets off a wardrobe, a chair, and an old chandelier.

Very cautiously, Mr. Driscoll draped the largest blanket over the dresser. That done, he tucked a second blanket along the bottom of the piece. "If I tilt it up, can you push the ends beneath it?" he asked, looking up at her.

She nodded. "Yes," Isabel added aloud, on the chance that he couldn't see the motion beneath the massive chapeau. Sending out two more puffs of smoke for good measure, she set aside the smoker. With her hands still tucked deep into her sleeves, she crouched beside the dresser. As soon as he tilted it the bees began humming again, and she hummed back at them as the old beekeeper in Florence used to do, trying to soothe the creatures, while she pushed the underside of the blanket as far as it would go. They switched places, and she pulled the end of the blanket out, pushing the nearer end under so they overlapped.

"Well done," he said, setting the bundled dresser flat again and placing another blanket over it for good measure. "They won't stay quiet for long, though." He walked to the door and tried to pull it open, only to have it yanked shut again from the other side. "For Christ's sa…" he began, glancing at her then back to the door again as he trailed off. "Send in three footmen," he ordered. "The bees are contained, but we need to get this dresser downstairs posthaste."

"Are you certain they're contained?" came the muffled query through the door.

The servants had closed her into the bee room right alongside her steward, Isabel realized. "The bees are contained," she stated, thankful they couldn't see her trying to sound authoritative in her absurd hat. They would never take her seriously if she attempted to command them while wearing that chapeau. "Come assist Mr. Driscoll at once."

The door inched open, the opening widening as no bees swarmed to attack. A trio of black-jacketed young men stumbled in, coughing at the haze of smoke and trying not to look either at her non-nakedness or at the hat, then took positions at three of the corners of the dresser and lifted. Driscoll gathered the hanging blanket ends and knotted them together, then took a corner for himself. The men headed, crablike and supremely careful, out the storage-room door.

"Are we to toss it in the lake?" one of them asked in a hushed voice as Isabel trailed them to the servants' stairs.

"No!" she exclaimed. Somewhere beyond her hearing she swore she heard her mother's voice and one of her fairy tales about the entire property at Nimway Hall being...sacred. Did that include the bees? "Put the dresser in the corner of the garden. Perhaps we could begin an apiary."

"I do like fresh honey," another of the young men stated, stumbling then righting himself, adding a colorful curse as their bundle hummed and vibrated in response.

"Steady," the steward said calmly, taking the backward position as they descended the stairs. Glancing up at Isabel, he smiled.

He had a good smile, she decided, and a rather attractive one that made her smile back at him – though he likely couldn't see her face through the heavy lace curtain of the hat. In fact, seeing her in the silly chapeau was likely the reason he was amused. Even given the item's absurdity, however, she had to acknowledge that lending it to her had been chivalrous, especially as stray bees continued to buzz about them.

Finally they reached the first floor, and crab-walked again down the back hallway to the rear of the house. Isabel moved ahead of them and threw open the back door, pressing herself against it as the men eased past her. They made their way around a wildly askew railing and down the shallow trio of steps into the simply-planted garden. Back behind a bed of likely-looking foxglove and hollyhocks, well off the pebble-covered walk, they set down the bundle.

"Thank you, lads," Driscoll said, squatting to unknot the tangle of blankets. "You'd all best get back inside. The bees likely aren't too happy at the moment."

The footmen practically fell over themselves in their haste to return to the Hall. If she hadn't been able to tell that they were genuinely worried about being stung, Isabel would have found the sight of flailing arms and flapping coat-tails horribly amusing.

"You as well, Miss de Rossi," her steward instructed.

"Yes, of course." Why was she still standing there in her night rail and robe anyway, gawping at a man wearing five jackets, at least four pairs of trousers, and she saw now, cravats tied at the base of his gloves and the tops of his boots? "Oh. Your hat." Swiftly she removed it, then settled it back on his black, wavy hair.

Her fingers brushed his jaw as she straightened the lace, tugging it down to cover his neck at the front and back. He had broad shoulders even without all the jackets, and her palm lingered, seemingly of its own accord, on the sun-warmed wool of the topmost jacket as she fiddled with the lace netting.

She didn't have much experience with Englishmen; from what she'd observed since her arrival in England, they carried themselves in a much more reserved manner than the men of Florence – but then she seemed to be related to half the men in Italy, so she couldn't judge a gentleman's actions by their teasing. This one appeared to be…competent, and not at all like one of the dandies illustrated in Mr. Cruikshank's drawings. But then Mr. Driscoll wasn't one of the London *haute ton*. Perhaps that was a good thing, because she certainly wouldn't have known how to talk to one of those creatures.

He cleared his throat, the hat tilting up again as he looked at her from his crouched position. "The bees'll be getting warm out here, and I can't help but think that won't be pleasant for me," he said, his voice pitched low to no doubt avoid further annoying their winged, humming captives.

Isabel shook herself, pulling her hand away from him. "Do be careful," she cautioned as she backed toward the steps. "Honey would be nice, but not at the expense of your good loo— your good health."

For heaven's sake, she'd nearly said his "good looks". To a man. A stranger. An employee. No one would see her as anything but a flighty, flirtatious, improper girl if she couldn't even mind her own tongue. Today, tomorrow – she only had a short time to make her first impression on her employees, tenants, and neighbors. She'd already scandalized Simmons by wearing a dressing robe to an emergency, but that didn't trouble her as much as the idea of Mr. Driscoll seeing her as a nodcock.

He waited until she stood in the back doorway with her hand on the door latch before he stood, slowly pulled off the blankets, and backed away.

For a moment everything remained still. Then bees began pouring from the dresser like black smoke. Driscoll continued to back away, more and more quickly, until abruptly he turned and ran – not for the house, but for the lake beyond the garden. Isabel watched, torn between alarm and admiration of his fine form, as he dove headfirst into the water.

Oh, dear. "Simmons," she called as she shut the door, only to turn around and walk straight into the butler's chest. "Oh! Please find me a blanket. And no one is to enter the garden until the bees have had time to settle."

"A blanket for you, Miss Isabel?" the butler returned, snapping his fingers at a maid, who hurried down the hallway. "I'm glad you've come to your senses and decided to cover yourself."

"It's not for me, Simmons," she returned, grateful her mother had warned her weeks ago about the stiff-spined butler. She'd lost the chance to impress him with her decorum – not that she possessed that in abundance – but she meant to win him over with her competence and compassion. And that began with seeing to her temporary steward.

"Of course it isn't," he said faintly, glowering toward the doorway.

She'd meant to sit down with Adam Driscoll immediately after breakfast this morning, meant to thank him for his service and send him on his way. Whether she had any experience managing an estate or not, she didn't want some stranger telling her what she should be doing. Particularly a stranger whom she hadn't hired herself. She knew perfectly well how to see to a household, and all she needed was a few days to find her footing here. And time to hire a steward of her own choosing, of course.

But now the steward had rescued a colony of bees for no other reason than that she'd asked him to do so. And he'd more than likely been stung in the process, *and* was presently paddling about in her lake while she waited in her silly night rail and robe to bring him a dry blanket. Oh, he probably thought her a complete fool. She certainly looked like one. But neither did she mean to leave him out there, soaking wet, while she donned proper clothes and put up her hair.

She shook herself again. Very well. Adam Driscoll's bravery combined with his absurd hat had earned him another day in her employ. She'd consider what to do with him again tomorrow.

CHAPTER 4

Myrrden Lake lay cool and deep and still around Adam as he warily surfaced. A dozen bees had taken the plunge with him, and they floated on the surface with a final defiant leg twitch or two that sent minute ripples out around them.

Despite the cold plunge, this morning had actually progressed much more smoothly than he'd expected. And that truly surprised him – especially with Isabel de Rossi entering the room in nothing but a robe and her night rail. Even with the thing buttoned up to her chin she'd looked…fetching, her dark hair loose around her shoulders and her hands tucked into the huge sleeves.

As that thought crossed his mind she appeared at the edge of the water to wave at him from beyond the boundary of the estate's garden. Adam lifted a hand in return, grabbed the hat which floated nearby, and dove to swim toward her. Quite a showing he'd made on her first full day at Nimway Hall. First trying to shove a valuable antique out the window, then ending up diving into the lake. *And* he wore multiple layers of clothes, currently trying to sink him, and had been caught wearing a modified woman's hat. What a literal stuffed buffoon he must look.

"Were you stung?" she asked, taking a step back from the shore as he emerged from the water. She held out a blanket as if she feared he'd shed his seventy pounds of sodden clothes and would be entirely nude.

"Once or twice," he returned, though he knew precisely that he'd been stung twice, once on each hand. These hurt like the devil, as had the stings he'd gotten two weeks ago when he'd last attempted the bee extermination. But he wasn't about to let her know that. Instead he took the blanket from her and ran it over his hair.

"Oh, dear. We should have some apple cider vinegar in the kitchen, shouldn't we?"

Adam tilted his head at her from beneath the edge of the blanket. "You know how to treat bee stings?"

Miss de Rossi smiled, and he amended his earlier assessment of her appearance. Even still wearing the puff-sleeved dressing robe she didn't just look fetching; she looked…attractive.

"Bees aren't exclusive to Somerset," she commented. "Florence is rife with them, as well." She gestured him toward the side of the house. "We had several apiaries, and some very fine honey."

"Florence, Italy?" he asked, shaking himself a little. He was her steward, dammit all. Ogling her was most definitely not professional.

"Yes. I grew up there."

That explained the slight accent in her otherwise flawless speech. It also explained a few other things. "De Rossi," he repeated. "Simmons told me that a famous Italian sculptor named de Rossi carved that rather impressive fireplace in the dining room. Any relation?"

Her smile deepened. Not just attractive, he amended again. Enchanting. "Marco de Rossi is my father. He and Mama eloped. The fireplace is in her image. It was very romantic."

Adam swallowed. The attractive, bare-chested lady carved into the fireplace was Isabel de Rossi's mother? He'd...touched the thing. In admiration of the artist's obvious skill, of course, but even so. And being Charlotte Harrington's parents, having to see that carving every time they sat down for a formal dinner? With guests? Was that why they'd retreated to London? He certainly couldn't blame them for that. But he wouldn't term anything that led to such a fine house being abandoned for ten years "romantic". "You've seen it, then?"

"Yes. The dining room was my first stop last night. I'd origi-nally planned to go back and look at the fireplace by daylight this morning," she continued blithely. "Detoured by bees."

Oh, yes. The bees. They'd nearly slipped his mind for some reason. "Thank you for your assistance with the little pests. I'd tried relocating them before, but they never cooperated until today. They would settle on the curtains, the furniture, us – anything but return to their hive." Adam grimaced. "I wouldn't have been willing to sacrifice the furniture if I hadn't attempted everything else first."

She flipped her hand. "I would rather lose a dresser than see anyone stung. But thank *you* for making another attempt to save the hive. And for jumping into the lake. If any of your...multitude of clothes are ruined, I will of course replace them."

A chuckle left his lips before he could remind himself that he was still attempting to make a competent first impression – and he'd already worn a woman's hat and taken a swim this morning. He was currently dripping lake water on the hem of her very puffy dressing gown at this very moment. "They aren't all my clothes. I borrowed from every large, burly man in the vicinity." He shrugged wetly. "It seemed to work, at least. The only stings are on my wrists, between the leather gloves and my sleeves."

He glanced at her again as she looked down at his still-gloved hands. This morning had by no means been a vision of clockwork and efficiency. It had been a bumbling bramble of confusion that by some miracle had ended with the preferred result. He'd thought to be sacked over it. Not praised as a hero.

"It was very clever. And so was that extremely unique hat."

"I found it in an attic room and added the lace myself. If it was something precious, I—"

"It was a hat," she broke in. "I daresay you had more use of it than whichever of my female ancestors purchased it."

From what little he knew of her grandmother, he doubted Olivia Harrington would have been as forgiving of all the chaos. "You managed the bees well."

She nodded. "We keep bees in Florence. I used to assist old Pietro when he removed the honeycombs. I haven't done it for years, though."

They reached the kitchen, and Miss de Rossi sent everyone into a whirlwind of activity – chasing after apple cider vinegar, dry clothes and boots for him, someone to tend to the wet clothes he wore, and Mrs. Dall, the cook, to brew him some hot tea.

They were an efficient household – Simmons saw to that – but Adam could swear the servants practically flew to see to Isabel de Rossi's orders in a way they never had for him. With this being by her own admission her first visit here, their immediate acceptance and apparent…joy at her arrival stunned him. Servants were always leery of change, and this was a huge change for them. Perhaps, though, they were merely trying to impress their new mistress.

She offered him a chair at the large kitchen table, pulling out the one beside it as well and turning the two to face each other. When she took the second seat and reached for his right hand, he frowned. "I can tend myself, Miss de Rossi. You do not need to—"

"You were injured beneath my roof," she countered calmly, her fine brow furrowing as she tugged on the damp knots of the old cravat he'd knotted around his forearm to keep bees from crawling all the way up his sleeves. "And you saved countless bee lives with your bravery. Do stop protesting."

"I… Very well." His mouth curved, and he didn't try to prevent it. "The bees might not see me as their rescuer, and I would tend to award you that honor anyway, but I'm pleased I at least made any onlookers laugh."

The sharp glance she sent him seemed to measure instantly whether he was jesting or not, then to approve with a warm twinkle and a wrinkled nose. "I shall commission a very tiny medal for you to wear on your lapel. A gold bee on a field of red, sword crossed with stinger."

Adam laughed. "Whether you manage that or not, in my mind I shall always be wearing it."

At the same time, he began to wonder whether he'd struck his head when he dove into the lake. He generally wasn't prone to silliness or flights of fancy. They didn't mesh well with keeping an estate – this estate, in particular – in good order. Bees currently resided in a chest of drawers in the garden. When Miss de Rossi heard about the rest of the Nimway disasters and what a poor showing he'd made in response to them, he doubted she would continue to be amused.

And if she *was* amused by a chipped millstone, broken garden railings, a slipping irrigation gate, and the other half a hundred things that needed tending, then she didn't belong there any more than he did.

Then she began to tug the glove off his hand, and he forgot what he'd been worrying over. Somewhere in the busy, logical back of his mind he did note that once Mrs. Dall set the bowl of vinegar and a cloth at her mistress's elbow the cook slipped out of the kitchen – and that every other servant had already done so.

What the devil? Properly-trained servants – which the employees of Nimway Hall had been up to this point – knew better than to leave a single woman alone in the presence of an unmarried man unless expressly ordered to do so. He certainly hadn't heard Miss de Rossi do so.

"You've been here for what, four weeks now?" she asked conversationally, dipping one corner of the cloth into the vinegar until it was well saturated, then holding out her free hand, palm up.

Taking in a slow breath through his nose, abruptly grateful to still be clothed in five layers of wet, uncomfortable trousers, he placed his hand in hers, palm down. She had a small hand, but her fingers were long and graceful and much softer than his rough ones. Her father was an artist, and he imagined she must be skilled in the arts, as well.

"Yes?" she prompted, placing the soaked cloth firmly against the tender, swollen back of his wrist.

The relief was almost instantaneous. What had she asked him, though? "Yes. Yes, four weeks. If I'd known you were coming, I would have prepared a written assessment already. I had intended to send one to Mrs. Harrington at the end of the month."

She nodded, her gaze on his hand. "Have you been everywhere?"

"'Everywhere?'" he repeated. "I've visited every farm, tenant, and every shop in Balesborough, East Pennard, and West Pennard. Except for the blacksmith in Balesborough. Apparently he went north for a sister's wedding. The—"

"I meant in the house," she broke in, her cheeks reddening a little. "Have you explored the house?"

"Of course. I only found one leak, in the corner of one of the attic rooms, and I regret to report that it has yet to be repaired. The bees were using it to enter and exit, I believe, and I didn't think it wise to trap them inside. Two doors are off plum, and one needs to be rehung, one window in the morning room is cracked, and three of them need re—"

"Did you see anything unusual?" she blurted, dipping the cloth in the apple cider vinegar again and reapplying it.

Adam lifted an eyebrow. She'd lowered her head, so he couldn't see her expression beneath the disheveled tumble of thick dark-brown hair. If he had to put a name to it, though, he would say she was embarrassed. Over what, though? "Unusual in what way?" he asked in return. "All in all I found Nimway and its environs to be in remarkably fine condition, if that's what you're asking. If not, you'll have to be more specific, Miss de Rossi."

She cleared her throat. "In my mother's time there was an... orb, I suppose, an oval-shaped moonstone of milky white, in a setting of gold eagle claws." She released the cloth and turned her hand palm up, forming her fingers into claws to demonstrate. "A little larger than my closed fist." Again she used her hand to demonstrate what she said. "Have you see that anywhere?"

Isabel held her breath as his pretty green eyes lost focus. Surely he'd seen the orb somewhere. If not, she would ask Simmons and, if need be, everyone else who lived within the Hall. The servants, though, would know the tales about it, and they would also know her reasons for wanting to find it. Even her no-nonsense grand-mother had acknowledged its existence and its power, and her mother had said the orb appeared when it should, where it should, and to whom it should.

"A crystal ball, you mean?" her steward asked, his large hand flexing a little in hers. "A gypsy's glass ball?"

"No, no. It's very old, and has been missing for some time." For nineteen years, actually, since it had shown Charlotte Harrington her true love, bound her to Marco de Rossi, then apparently vanished without a trace.

But she wasn't Charlotte. She was Isabel, and now it was her turn. She'd come to be the Hall's guardian, not just because of the romance of it all, but because Nimway had been without a mistress for ten years. That couldn't be allowed to continue. Her ancestral home needed a descendant to live here. She would take care of Nimway Hall. And if she happened to be here without a suitor in sight, well, perhaps in return the Hall would take care of her. There didn't quite seem to be rules, or at least not any that she knew about, but since well before her five-times great grand-mother the Hall and its guardian had watched over each other. She was here to do her part. Therefore, the magic would happen. She only needed to wait for it – and to find the orb.

"I don't recall seeing any such thing," Mr. Driscoll replied unhelpfully.

Isabel sighed. "No, I don't suppose you would have." Lifting the cloth from his hand, she decided the swelling had subsided enough that she could remove his other glove to see to the nearly identical sting on the back of his left wrist.

The stinger remained in this one, and she sent him a sympathetic grimace before she scraped it out with her fingernails, careful not to pinch more venom beneath his skin. The steward didn't even flinch. From his appearance last evening, he undoubtedly wrestled wild beasts on a regular basis, but she'd been stung before, and it had hurt.

"I'd wondered," he said into the silence, "why Nimway Hall has been unoccupied for so long. It's a fairly large holding, and from what your grandmother's solicitor wrote, the owners haven't lived here for ten years."

"We had a steward," she returned, reminding herself that she needed to sack this one and choose her own as soon as possible. "But yes, he became a little...negligent in his later months. Honestly, I think the fireplace carving made my grandparents uncomfortable. They're very English."

He chuckled. "I sense that isn't a compliment."

Oh dear, she probably shouldn't have said that. "I agree that Nimway shouldn't have been abandoned for so long. It has guardians, and a guardian should always be here to look after it. My mother would have been, except that...circumstances led her to Florence." Circumstances that included parents who thought she'd married below her station, a previously-arranged marriage, and Charlotte's need to be free.

As a consequence Isabel had lived an unrestrained childhood, running about with the children of other artists, sitting for huge, informal dinners where everyone was a storyteller, and daydreaming about the magical castle awaiting her back in England. It had also left her considering that with her bohemian upbringing, she needed a husband who knew the rules, knew how to behave like an English gentleman, and could provide her with the decorum that had clearly been missing from her lessons. Knowing how to smoke bees was well and good, but that was a very different task from hosting a proper dinner or attending a proper soiree.

"You mean to remain here, then?" he asked, shaking her out of her reverie again.

"I do. For the rest of my life." She lifted her chin a little, waiting for him to question whether she'd be lonely or if she knew what she was getting into. When he didn't reply, Isabel took a short breath. "My parents can come see me, and my grandparents are just in London."

Yes, it already felt very different from the rambling house in Florence, where friends and family always filled the halls and laughter and song and conversation lasted well into the night. But this was *her* place, *her* adventure, and she couldn't wait for it to begin.

"You've taken on quite a task," he finally commented. "I'd be pleased to show you my points of concern and, of course, where I've kept the accounts ledgers and my observational notes."

She looked up from his hand to find him gazing at her, though he lowered his eyes the moment she met them. No doubt he found her too young and too ridiculous and sentimental – she'd saved bees, after all – for the responsibility of Nimway Hall. Yes, the house in Florence had been smaller and with fewer assets and no tenants.

At least she was aware of that, and perhaps she would make use of him until she caught up. He could just enlighten her until she took over his job or found someone else who could – someone who would answer to her rather than to her grandmother. That all sounded horrible even in her own head, though; she wasn't precisely ruthless. Perhaps a week would give her enough time to figure all this out. She did owe him for the bee stings, at the least.

"Thank you," she said aloud, offering her best smile. "I would very much appreciate it."

Abruptly Mr. Driscoll cleared his throat, pulling his hand from between hers. "Thank *you* for your ministrations, but I need to shed some layers of clothing and head to the mill. The runner stone is chipped, and I've held the stonemason here for an additional day already." He stood, collecting the wet gloves and ruined cravats. "If you'll excuse me, Miss de Rossi?"

This millstone would be one of her responsibilities once he was gone. It was one of them *now*, actually. "I'll accompany you," she decided, setting aside the vinegar and rising, as well.

"There was a mishap yesterday. Someone might have been hurt. If you—"

"I'll risk it," she interrupted. "Give me a moment to dress, Mr. Driscoll."

"Adam," he countered. "My oldest brother is Mr. Driscoll."

Isabel inclined her head. "Adam, then," she said, trying not to notice how well his name sat on her tongue. Nimway Hall might have a husband in mind for her, but it wouldn't be one of her own employees. Someone not only knowledgeable about Society, but more than likely titled – that sounded much more fitting for the spouse of the Hall's guardian. She loved her father, but a foreign sculptor? She wouldn't be making that mistake. With the shortcomings she already had, she wouldn't be doing anything to add to them.

As soon as she left the kitchen she gathered the skirts of her night rail and robe in her fists and raced up the stairs. Jane was still nowhere to be seen, so she ran back one door down from her large bedchamber to the room her past nanny and present companion had taken.

"Jane," she called, knocking, then pushing open the door and walked into the room. "Are you still asleep? I must dress! Hurry!"

The older woman gave a broken snore and sat straight up. "The rabbits are loose!" she muttered, flailing at her disheveled red-gray hair, presently wrapped about her head like a shroud.

"There are no rabbits," Isabel said calmly, walking over to throw open the curtains.

"What? Where are they?"

"Only in your dream." Waking Jane Davies from a sound sleep

had once been one of Isabel's favorite guilty pleasures; the woman evidently had very vivid – and unusual – dreams. "We did catch a beehive in the attic and transport it out to the garden. Mr. Driscoll – Adam – was stung twice."

"Oh, my," Jane said, wrestling free of her hair and the bed sheets. "Is he allergic? I had a second cousin who perished from a bee sting."

"He's fine. I put a cloth soaked in apple cider vinegar on the stings. But we're off to the mill, and I cannot go in my night clothes."

Jane froze, swiveling around to stare at her. "Your night clothes? Oh, good heavens. You – the servants – you were outside in your night clothes?"

"People were yelling," Isabel explained, deciding she was being quite patient. "I couldn't take the time to dress."

"Please don't ever tell your grandmother about this," her companion urged, crossing herself. "She thinks I'm too indulgent as it is." To hear Jane Davies tell it, her family had been so Catholic they'd had to flee England for Italy. Isabel actually thought their flight from Bristol had had more to do with the grandfather's gambling debts, but she would never say such a thing to Jane.

"I am trying, Jane," Isabel returned. "The idea of having someone about who would yell at me makes me shudder."

"Me, as well. No more going about in your night rail, Isabel." Straightening her own voluminous night rail, Jane shooed Isabel out of the room and followed her into the master bedchamber. "Curse my sound sleeping. Next time you must wake me." Jane dug into one of the trunks that hadn't yet been unpacked. "Your green muslin?"

"Where's my riding habit? I imagine Adam means to ride, and I doubt there's a rig I can drive. We must purchase one."

"But you cannot go riding alone with a man, Isabel. This isn't Florence, and Mr. Driscoll isn't one of your cousins. And you shouldn't be addressing him as Adam."

"He asked me to. And one of the grooms is accompanying us,

of course," Isabel decided, making a mental note to request one. She'd thought an isolated estate in the middle of rural Somerset would be a bit less tricky to navigate than London, but given nearly everyone's reaction this morning, she'd misjudged. In fact, Adam – Mr. Driscoll – was the only one who *hadn't* gawked at her for not taking time to dress.

They found her riding boots and the two-piece habit of deep forest green. She'd never worn this one; a wool riding dress was far too warm for Italian summers. Thankfully it fit as well as it had when she'd tried it on at the dressmaker's a month ago.

The moment Jane finished pinning up her hair and set the matching green hat artfully askew atop that, Isabel hurried back downstairs. Simmons stood, also completely dressed and much more composed looking, in the foyer. "Have I beaten Mr. Driscoll?" she asked, as she pulled on her black leather riding gloves.

The old butler lifted an eyebrow. "If you were engaged in a race, Miss Isabel, you have lost. The...fellow went out to the stables five minutes ago."

"'The fellow'?" she repeated. "Do you dislike Adam?" If Simmons knew something that would make sacking the steward easier, she certainly wanted to know about it.

"He's not from here."

The way he spoke the words said that that explanation should be more than enough to suffice, but Isabel frowned. "I'm not from here, either."

"You were born elsewhere, Miss Isabel," Simmons countered in his dry voice. "You are most certainly *from* here. More so than anyone else beneath this roof." He leaned a breath closer. "And if I may be so bold, we are all very happy to have you here finally. Nimway needs her guardian."

Now *this* was the greeting she'd wanted. An affirmation that the house – and the household – were pleased she'd come home, even if she'd never been there before. "Thank you, Simmons. I'm very happy to be here."

And she would be even happier when she had a moment to walk the rest of the house by herself, to let the peace of this place wash over her, and to find that blasted orb so she could begin the task of finding the man with whom she was meant to share Nimway Hall and her new life.

CHAPTER 5

"*A* bit more, lads," the stonemason instructed, leaning down to peer at the narrowing gap between the runner stone and the bed stone. "Gently now, or we'll have to start all over again."

As Adam let out another inch of rope, he sent yet another glance at Miss de Rossi to make certain she was well clear of any potential accident. She'd donned a dark-green riding habit that hugged her curves in a way he couldn't help noticing. In fact, he almost preferred the night rail, which had at least been oversized and covered with a robe. Tom Reynolds the stonemason had been spending more time than necessary eyeing her, as well, and had taken it upon himself to explain every known fact about millstones, how he'd repaired this one, and which other estates he'd evidently saved from devastation by virtue of his skill.

With a ton of stone at the end of the rope and five other men helping him hold it aloft, there wasn't a great deal Adam could do about the mason's prattling. The worst bit was that Isabel – Miss de Rossi – seemed supremely interested in what Reynolds had to say.

Adam couldn't decide quite what to make of her. If he owned an estate as grand as Nimway Hall he wouldn't have been able to stay away, either. But she was young and, from her questions, didn't have much in the way of practical world knowledge. And while he would have been willing to wager that she had some experience running a household, Nimway was much more than that.

At the same time, though, she seemed very willing to learn, and he hadn't been able to detect an ounce of haughtiness about her. She'd walked into a room full of annoyed bees, had found a way to save the hive, and had not only known the remedy for bee stings but had applied it herself. And she had no difficulty encouraging the mundane tales of a self-important stonemason.

These men at the mill had reacted with the same relief and happiness upon seeing her that the Nimway servants had shown. They'd only just begun voluntarily speaking to *him*, and that had been after a month of hard work. Yet there she was, freshly arrived with nothing to recommend her but her parentage, and the locals couldn't wait to introduce themselves.

Yes, she was pretty – stunningly so – with her long dark hair swept up beneath an impractical green hat and eyes the color of a restless sea, but Adam had the distinct feeling that she could have been a peg-legged, one-eyed gargoyle, and her tenants would have welcomed her with the same fervor. Why, though? They'd all fared well over the past ten years, even with a neglectful, fading steward and no landowner present on the property. The house itself had suffered the most, and even that – in the greater scheme of things – was fairly negligible.

As the stonemason launched into a lecture concerning imported French runner stones, the said stone settled back into place, and the rest of them let the rope go slack. Adam shook out his arms. "Before we return Mr. Reynolds to Glastonbury, we should give the millstone a turn or two. Mr. Miller?"

The miller nodded. Once they freed the runner stone from the ropes, he and his son pulled the heavy lever to reconnect the mechanism to the water wheel outside. He fed in a sackful of seed, and a moment later the ancient mill groaned into motion.

A few tense turns passed before the miller retrieved a handful of the milled seed, ground into a rough white powder. "She'll do," he pronounced with a pleased grin. "We're set for the harvest, Miss Isabel."

The owner of Nimway Hall stepped forward to sweep the grain from the miller's hand and inspect it for herself. "Well done, all of you. And Mr. Miller, please let me know when you would be available to help me learn the mechanics of the process, and if there's anything more you require."

"I'd be honored, Miss Isabel."

The stonemason opened his mouth, no doubt to offer his own expertise, and Adam stepped forward. "I need to ride into Balesborough to order new railing for the rear stairs leading into the garden. Do you wish to accompany me, Miss de Rossi? Or is there something else you'd prefer to see?" He'd meant to have most of the repairs seen to by the time anyone came to reside in the great house, but weather and circumstances had had other ideas. And if she wished to view any more – or all – of his failings, it was certainly her right to do so.

"I shall join you, Adam," she returned, and with another smile and nod for the gathered men, she led the way outside.

"—knew she'd arrived before word came down from the Hall," a low voice said from the mill behind him, and Adam slowed his exit.

"Aye. The owls," Phillip Miller returned, even more quietly. "There were butterflies all over Agnes's pen this morning, as well. Flew off and settled like a blue and red and yellow blanket on the knapweed along the stream. Never seen the like."

From all the affirmative grunting, Adam gathered that the owls and butterflies had portended something significant. He'd heard the owls, an entire parliament of them, but he'd put it to a well-lit coach passing through Balesboro Wood to disturb their twilight hunting. And everyone knew butterflies liked knapweed.

But villagers liked their superstitions, and as long as they didn't interfere with his work, he had no objections.

As he left the mill to take in the sight beside the millstream, however, he didn't feel quite as magnanimous. Someone had alerted the vultures in addition to the owls and butterflies. "Lord Alton," he intoned, as his jaw clenched. "What brings you all the way up from Blackbridge?"

Alton released Isabel's black-gloved fingers and straightened. "Driscoll," he drawled. "Nimway Hall has a new mistress. Naturally I had to come and meet her." He smiled down at Isabel. "Introduce us properly, will you?"

Adam would rather have flattened the man, but punching the Viscount Alton today would only get him sacked. "Alton, Miss de Rossi. Isabel, Geoffrey Bell-Spratt, Viscount Alton. He owns Blackbridge Abbey, just south of Wells."

"And Alton Park, in the Lake District," Alton added, sketching a bow. "I much prefer Blackbridge, though. The views here are much more fine."

Isabel's already tanned cheeks darkened. "Finer than the views of the Lake District? You flatter me, my lord."

"That was my aim, Isabel. I may call you Isabel, I hope? And you must call me Geoffrey. We are neighbors, after all."

And I live in the damned house with her, Adam pointed out silently, but they seemed to have forgotten he stood there. He watched as she inclined her head. "You may, Geoffrey. I'm glad to meet one of my neighbors."

Someone must have sent word to Blackbridge of Miss de Rossi's arrival very early this morning in order for Alton to have ridden the two hours it would take to reach Nimway Hall by luncheon. Adam drew a breath. Isabel was young, unmarried, and with a large property in her name. It made sense she would have gentlemen callers. It was certainly no business of his if she did. No doubt Alton was only the first; the other neighbors would be flocking to Nimway Hall, as well. And Alton had never passed up an opportunity to make an advantageous acquaintance.

Adam found himself gazing at Alton's spine as the viscount turned his back. Geoffrey Bell-Spratt could pretend they were barely acquainted if he wished, but Adam damned well remembered the last time they'd met. He was tempted to mention it. Only two things stopped him. First, he had been raised to follow the tenets of gentlemanly behavior, and a gentleman didn't intentionally embarrass anyone. Second, even he had to concede that character could change a great deal in six years. His had.

And if for a moment he wished the ladies didn't find Geoffrey Bell-Spratt quite so pretty, that could be excused. Miss de Rossi had said she'd spent very little time in London. She wouldn't have much experience, then, with the likes of Alton. On principle he didn't approve of rakes in general. From experience he didn't like Bell-Spratt in particular.

Alton turned half around, and those blue eyes that ladies sighed over slanted in Adam's direction. "Off to Balesborough, are you?" the viscount drawled. "I'm certain Driscoll doesn't mind me tagging along."

Driscoll *did* mind, but he would tolerate it if Isabel agreed to it. "There are people you should meet in the village, Miss de Rossi. We can of course make your introductions later, if you wish."

"Would these people be alarmed to have Lord Alton included in these introductions?"

He stifled a sigh. "No. I have no reason to think so."

She smiled. "Balesborough it is, then."

Adam nodded. "We'd best be off. Billy, bring the horses around, would you?"

"Aye, Mr. Driscoll," the groom said, hurrying back around the side of the mill where they'd left his chestnut and the black filly Miss de Rossi had claimed. When he came back around, Adam stepped forward to boost Isabel into the saddle before Alton could do so.

"You look like you swallowed a bee," she murmured, shifting her skirt to step into his cupped hands. "I'm to be wary of Lord Alton, I presume?"

Surprised at her perceptiveness, Adam looked up at her as she settled into the side saddle. "I..." He swallowed back the comment he'd been about to make. "You'll have to form your own opinion, Miss de Rossi. I will only say that he is known to have expensive tastes, and you have a prosperous estate."

It didn't feel gentlemanly to say that last bit, but if Isabel had grown up here or in London, she would have been aware of Alton's wildly fluctuating finances and his reputation. She shouldn't be at a disadvantage; nor would she be, while he remained as her steward.

She thanked him with a slight nod before he turned to claim the chestnut. Isabel understood his warning; Lord Alton was seeking a way to increase his finances. Thanks to a very insightful ancestor she would never have to worry about losing Nimway Hall to a husband or a son, but a reckless guardian or spouse could do a great deal of damage to the property's finances, regardless. Not that Lord Alton had done anything more than appear and invite himself along to the nearest village, but both her mother and her grandmother had warned her that the moment a man learned she had wealth and property, he would be interested.

The trick, she supposed, would be to find one of those interested men who interested her, in turn. And for that she could certainly use the orb – wherever it might be. She bore a birthmark in its shape on the back of her left shoulder, but she couldn't very well go about baring her skin to say, "look for this somewhere on the property". But the mark had significance even if she couldn't show it to anyone else – it told *her* that she belonged here. And today, that nearly felt like enough.

They headed along the rutted road toward Balesborough, and she found herself between Adam and the viscount. Lord Alton was on his third amusing tale about someone he knew from London, while her steward seemed content to look handsome as he rode silently at her side. While the two men were of similar size and build, in everything else she didn't think they could have appeared more different. The viscount sported high collars and a precisely-tied cravat, and his light-blue coat and matching blue beaver hat, gray trousers, and brown waistcoat embroidered with tiny yellow flowers looked well fitted and supremely expensive. She could see her distorted reflection in his tassled Hessian boots.

Adam, on the other hand, had donned worn buckskins with scuffed boots, his coat and waistcoat of an unremarkable brown that fit, but would barely be passable at a tavern, much less at a proper gathering. His cravat was clean if simply tied, and he'd neglected to wear a hat at all. From his tanned face, this wasn't the first time he'd forgone headwear.

Isabel shook herself. It didn't signify what her steward wore. He was her employee, a man clearly accustomed to hauling on ropes and running from angry bees. While she wasn't a titled lady, titles had come and gone in her family tree, and she'd grown up knowing that she was a part of the aristocracy. And yes, she anticipated finding her true love and marrying. That didn't necessarily mean Lord Alton. It certainly didn't mean Adam Driscoll. The orb would know, if she found a blasted minute to go look for it.

In her daydreams of her first day at Nimway Hall, the orb had appeared in her bedchamber, as it had been wont to do with her predecessors over the decades. It would somehow point her in the direction of her future husband, then she would know how to proceed. Instead of an orb, though, she'd had bees and a millstone. She took a deep breath. Both had been important, and both had been dealt with. This afternoon, after she returned from Balesborough, she would set aside the time to make a much more in-depth tour of the house. Because that was important, too – just on a much more personal level.

As Lord Alton opened his mouth to begin a fourth tale of London misadventures, she leaned forward to pat the pretty black filly on the withers. "I've decided to name my mare Fiore. That's Italian for—"

"For *flower*, if I remember my Italian," the viscount interrupted. "Very appropriate. A flower for a lovely flower."

She smiled. "Thank you. "What's your mount's name?"

"Staffordshire in the Morning Light," he replied promptly. "Stafford for short."

"Ah. Very regal sounding."

"He's a cousin to Master Jackey, winner of the first Royal Ascot Gold Cup."

The Royal Ascot. That was a prestigious race here in England, if she recalled correctly. Lord Alton seemed to think very highly of it, anyway. "Marvelous," she said. That sounded appropriate.

On her other side Adam made a low sound in his chest. *Derision?* She looked at him. "And what is your horse's name? He's very handsome."

He lifted an eyebrow, his expression equal parts amused and baffled. "Boy, I suppose," he returned. "Or Horse."

"He doesn't have a name?" Now *she* felt baffled. Goodness, she named everything, including Tinker, the little mouse that lived behind the stove in Florence; Fluff and Squawk, the chickens; and Bach, the bluebird, who'd made a nest outside her old bedchamber window.

"You, sir," Lord Alton commented, "suffer from a singular lack of imagination."

"I received the offer of a position, I purchased a mount as I had been using one of the horses from my uncle's property, and I rode here. He's a steady, deep-chested animal, but I've had other concerns."

"How very single-minded of you," the viscount complimented, in the least complimentary-sounding tone ever.

That was mean. "In all honesty, my lord," she noted, "you didn't name your mount, either, did you?"

The viscount smiled, attractive and amused. "True enough. I did select one with a bloodline and a name, however. Heritage matters."

Behind her, Adam snorted. "Now you've insulted Miss de Rossi, who has just selected a mare and named her without knowing her bloodline. Well done, Alton."

"I don't believe you're permitted to speak to me that way, Driscoll."

Adam opened his mouth, no doubt about to challenge Lord Alton's view of himself. "Oh, for heaven's sake," Isabel said, before either could question the other's masculinity, "you" – and she pointed at the steward – "work for me. And you" – and she pointed at the viscount – "are, I assume, attempting to charm me or something of the like. Behave, and show me the sights of my property, or leave and I'll see to it myself."

Lord Alton inclined his head. "Speak with me later if you'd like a recommendation for a proper steward. I believe I could suggest several who would never consider speaking out of turn."

Isabel didn't reply to that. How could she? Firstly, she meant to choose her own man. And secondly, any affirmation would serve to notify Adam Driscoll that he was on the verge of being removed. And at this moment, she needed him. Over the past few hours observing his precise expertise at the mill and his obvious knowledge of Nimway Hall, she'd realized that she couldn't allow her own sense of…destiny, she supposed it was, to blind her to the fact that she didn't know how to do a great deal of this. Repairing a vital mill wasn't the same as organizing and scheduling the household's meals for the week.

That realization only strengthened as she stood close enough to the blacksmith's forge to feel its heat and listened to Adam and Joseph Coopering discuss iron content and base depth for the replacement railing. In fact, the entire discussion left her rather light-headed and short of breath. What if her grandmother hadn't hired Mr. Driscoll to replace old Prentiss? She'd been a naïve fool to think she could arrive at Nimway and magically everything would sort itself out. Smithing wasn't magic. It was mathematics and hard work. The same with the millstone.

"…meet me for luncheon on Wednesday?" Lord Alton was saying, and she shook herself.

"I've only just arrived, my lord," she returned, trying not to squeak in surprise. "I would greatly appreciate a week or two to sort myself out before I ride off to luncheon." For heaven's sake, she wanted a moment to breathe before men began flinging themselves at her – if that was what this was. It felt like it. Abruptly she wished she'd taken her grandmother's advice and attended at least one party in London. Or that she'd gone to finishing school. Anything to help her not to feel like a halfwit when a gentleman asked her to luncheon.

Geoffrey's engaging smile returned. "If it takes a fortnight for your steward to catch you up on the state of Nimway Hall, at the risk of repeating myself I'd venture to say you need a new steward."

She sent a quick glance at Adam's broad back, but he gave no indication that he'd heard a word of the viscount's assessment. It was an unkind thing to say aloud, regardless. She certainly had no idea yet whether Adam Driscoll knew what he was doing or not, but "incompetent" was not the first – or the second or the third – word she conjured when she looked at him. Whatever else he was, though, he was her employee, and therefore under her protection.

"If you continue to insult my steward, my lord, I will have to assume you are also insulting me." No, she hadn't hired Adam Driscoll, but Grandmama Olivia had.

"I wouldn't dream of insulting you, Isabel. I see, though, that I've put a foot off the path. I therefore apologize. And I'll take my leave while you're impressed with my humility." Geoffrey swept a bow that she imagined would have been judged spectacular even by the members of the royal court, then exited the barn-like blacksmith's shop.

Isabel looked at the door through which he'd exited. Yes, he was charming. Yes, his…self-assurance left her a little unsettled. She'd instantly rebuffed any potential suitors since her fifteenth birthday, because she'd known since she could remember that she would be leaving Florence for Somerset as soon as she could do so, and she doubted any Italian count would wish to abide at an estate owned and managed by his wife.

But this *was* Somerset, and Lord Alton clearly knew who she was and what she owned. It all felt horribly confusing. In that sense, she'd meant what she said; she required more than twenty-four hours to find her footing here. And she'd been silly to expect an instant recognition and affinity.

The conversation behind her had ceased, she realized, and Isabel turned around to see Adam gazing at her, a quizzical expression on his lean face. *Wonderful*. Now she was daydreaming through conversations to which she should be paying attention. Isabel grimaced. "I beg your pardon?"

"We seem to have lost a viscount," he observed.

"I think he was bored. And I declined an invitation to luncheon with him on Wednesday." Why she added that last bit she wasn't certain, but as Adam nodded and gestured her toward the door, she had the feeling that he approved.

"I have several other things to see to, but it occurs to me that you haven't had much of an opportunity to walk your own floors at Nimway. Shall we return?"

"Yes, of course," she said, following him out the door. She certainly had dozens more people to meet, but as she kept reminding herself, she meant to be there for a very long time. Aside from that, hopefully learning the layout of her own home would help settle her thoughts and give her a chance to find her feet again. She was in over her head, and she disliked the sensation of drowning.

Before she could settle into self-pity, Adam put his hands around her waist and lifted her onto Fiore. Thank heavens her grandmother had hired someone to replace Prentiss. Because if the only magic Nimway Hall could provide was pretty sunrises, she definitely needed him here. And if she'd begun to feel a bit... thankful that Mr. Driscoll was lean and fit and handsome, well, she would simply appreciate the view until she found the orb and the man with whom she would share her life.

CHAPTER 6

"Why are we back in the library?" Jane asked, plunking herself into a chair with a groan.

"Because we've been everywhere else," Isabel returned absently, going up on her toes to see the back of the top shelves, opposite. No orb yet, dash it all. "And the library is the heart of a home, don't you think?"

"The heart of the house in Florence was the kitchen, if you ask me." Jane reached over to lift a book off the table beside her. "Someone's been reading about varieties of grain."

That would be Adam, no doubt. It felt odd, knowing he'd been living in her home for weeks before she'd ever arrived. The servants had been there as well, of course, but that was different. Simmons's employment could be measured in decades. Adam Driscoll, on the other hand, was new. New to Somerset, new to Nimway, and new to the unusual mythology of this land. And since he evidently read treatises on grain in his spare time when countless volumes about the Knights of the Round Table, Merlin, and Arthur abounded, she had her doubts about how...open-minded he would be if he discovered that all those ancient stories were true.

Most of them were true, anyway. Or based on truths. She was the most recent in a long line of female guardians of this place. And yes, she'd expected to find some evidence of her...specialness by now. In fact, now might be a good moment to test that.

Closing her eyes, she summoned and held onto the thought of the orb, about how smooth the stone must be, how bright the golden claws, how much she needed it to show her the path to her future. Then she held out one hand and turned a slow circle. When her position felt...right, she stepped forward, eyes still shut and finger outstretched, until her finger poked cloth.

Not the cloth that bound books, though. She opened her eyes to find herself gazing at a waistcoat. "I'm sorry to intrude," Adam Driscoll said, his own lowered gaze on the finger presently jabbed into his chest.

Her cheeks heated as she swiftly bent her finger into a fist and lowered it to her side. What an idiot she must have looked like. "I was... Oh, bother."

Adam lifted an eyebrow. "You certainly don't need to explain anything; this is your home," he said crisply. "Please inform me when you have a moment, and I'll—"

"I didn't mean you were bothering me," Isabel cut in. "Because you weren't. You aren't. I was...embarrassed because you caught me acting like a ninny, which is something I generally try to avoid."

His expression warmed. "I saw nothing the least bit ninny-like. I saw only a young woman becoming acquainted with her home."

Well, she could dispute that, but it wouldn't have been in her best interest to do so. "Thank you for saying that. What did you need?"

As she mustered her courage enough to look him in the eye again, his gaze lifted abruptly to meet hers. He'd been looking at her mouth, she realized, a different kind of heat flowing through her. Did he like her mouth? Had he been thinking of kissing her? Isabel shook herself again. *Stop being such a nodcock*, she ordered.

"It's not important," he returned. "Simmons said you'd gone

into the library, and I thought you might find this useful." He lifted a thick book in one hand and held it out to her. "I was looking for a good treatise on wheat. If you require anything, I'll be at the back of the house breaking up cement. Miss de Rossi." Inclining his head, he turned back for the door.

Isabel looked at the book he'd given her and flipped it open. In the neat cursive of at least a dozen different hands, it listed books, noting when they'd been acquired, which printed edition they might be, and where in the library they were located. One title immediately caught her eye: "Gathered Notes on the Oral History of Merlin's Staff and Headpiece". The orb was rumored to be a staff headpiece. Merlin's staff. *Good heavens.* In a sense, she *had* found the orb with her silly spinning and pointing. "Isabel," she said aloud, lifting her gaze to Adam's retreating backside.

He stopped, facing her. "I beg your pardon?"

"You gave me leave to call you Adam," she returned, trying not to sound as rushed and breathless as she abruptly felt. "It's only fair you should call me Isabel in return."

A slight smile curved his practical mouth. "Isabel, then."

The compilation of notes about the orb was, of course, missing, but at this moment that didn't seem to be the point. Magic was afoot here. She merely needed to figure out how to harness it. And how to stop feeling attracted to an employee.

This was her time, her chance, and while she was beginning to realize that running the household in Florence had been a great deal less complicated than Nimway was turning out to be, it had been a good foundation for what she needed to learn. In other ways, though, her upbringing had left her horribly ill-equipped for being the mistress of an estate. Unlike her mother, she meant to make a match with a proper gentleman. Yes, her parents adored each other, but that was them. Charlotte Harrington at least had had a proper upbringing and had, as odd as it seemed, made an educated, informed choice when she'd fallen in love with Marco de Rossi.

Isabel's own upbringing had been much less...structured, and filled with artists who, horror of horrors, worked for a living – often for wealthy patrons, as contracted employees. She needed to choose more sensibly than her mother had, because she had a great deal more to prove. And a handsome titled and propertied gentleman like Lord Alton made a great deal more sense than her own steward.

Now all she needed was to find the orb and wait for it to agree with her thinking.

~

ADAM DIDN'T WANT to go outside and break up the brittle cement that had finally set around the warped, wildly askew railing. He wanted to follow Isabel about the house as she looked for a crystal ball. Of course he didn't own this place, and he'd only invested a month in Nimway's upkeep, but he enjoyed seeing the genuine joy with which she viewed Nimway Hall. He liked it here; from the moment he'd arrived to see the forest and the meadows, the farms and the streams, he'd felt as though he was home.

That sense of…peace very nearly made him forget how poorly most of his endeavors had gone where the property was concerned. But as enthusiastic as Isabel had been, eventually she would notice his failures – which gave him a very limited amount of time to correct them. At least his last attempt at bee removal had gone well, as had the millstone's repair; with her present, any disaster, any misstep, would have been a glaringly obvious black mark on his chances of continued employment.

Retrieving his gloves from the small spare room where he'd moved most of his paperwork – he couldn't very well continue to utilize the office now that the mistress of the house was in residence – he pulled them on and went to join the pair of workers he'd hired from Balesborough.

He lifted a heavy pickax and went to work demolishing the railing support they'd attempted to pour nearly a month ago. Adam didn't like failures, especially when he had, as far as he could figure, done precisely what he should have done. Failures, missteps, cost time and money that belonged to someone else – in this instance, Isabel de Rossi.

He'd also discovered just this morning that Blackbridge Abbey wasn't as far away as he'd hoped, and that his dislike for Bell-Spratt hadn't lessened with time. It was obviously mutual, given the way the prissy, high-handed lord had immediately begun trying to sabotage his employment behind his back. Aside from their personal animosity, it rankled that Alton felt perfectly comfortable flirting and boasting while someone else saw to his responsibilities at his own estates. Geoffrey Bell-Spratt, Lord Alton, was a damned hypocritical ass.

He swung the pickax alongside the workers until sweat began to trickle down his back, at which point he stripped off his shirt and continued swinging. He couldn't make Alton go away, and his own gentleman's code prevented him from disparaging another man without the ass being there to defend himself, but he could bloody well pretend the lumps of cement were the viscount's smug face.

But the viscount owned a title and property. Isabel – and he liked saying her name, even to himself – owned property. That made her and Alton compatible. In the seven years he'd worked as a steward he'd never resented anyone for the blessings of luck or birth that granted property.

This was the first time it had ever struck him that he was an employee. This wasn't just helping out his uncle and realizing how much he enjoyed the work. He had to prove himself and be successful at his tasks, or he would find himself unemployed.

And he knew why it frustrated him now, why it abruptly mattered. Isabel de Rossi had had a safe, comfortable life in which she was no doubt adored by family and friends alike. And she'd chosen to come here, to a place she'd never been, with only a lady's companion to support her. True, her knowledge of the place and how to manage it were limited, but that gave him a reason to be there.

He could name two dozen property owners of his own acquaintance who had no idea what they were doing. He'd seen estates brought to ruin out of sheer arrogance and ignorance. Isabel seemed to want to learn, and while his opinion might be clouded by pretty gray eyes and an engaging smile, he would give her all the assistance he could. Even if it might eventually cost him his position.

"Mr. Driscoll?"

Blinking sweat from his eyes, Adam looked at his workmen, realizing at the same moment that the sun was a mere sliver on the horizon. How damned long had he been smashing cement in the dusk? "Let's continue this tomorrow, shall we?" he suggested, uncurling his fingers with some difficulty from the handle of the pickax. He would have blisters to keep his bee stings company tomorrow.

"Aye," the older one, Stephens, replied. "I've no wish to chop my own toes off in the dark."

Adam nodded. "Thank you, lads. We've made a good start."

"I think that was mostly you, Mr. Driscoll, but you're welcome. My boy and I'll be back first thing."

They tossed their tools into a wheelbarrow and headed off on the mile-long trek back to Balesborough. Adam looked up at the well-lit house. They would be sitting down for dinner soon, and he badly needed a bath. Hot water at dinnertime, though, was a rare commodity. He looked down at the lake just beyond the garden. Hell, he'd already swum in there once this week. Twice wouldn't hurt anything.

After retrieving his shirt and making a wide circuit around the bee chest just in case the insects hadn't yet settled in for the evening, he moved along the shore away from the house. Once he felt well hidden by the deepening shadows of the heavy undergrowth along the bank, he shucked out of his boots and trousers and dove in.

The shock of cold water actually felt good against his hot skin, and he dove down to touch the muddy bottom before he surfaced.

The moon had risen early, its reflection a wide, white path on the still water, one that led to the edge of the thick woods beyond the lake and vanished into inky darkness. A path to beckon the adventurous.

"And now you're becoming poetical," he muttered at himself. "That's not good."

Diving again, he stroked toward the shore. Once he surfaced he had to brush hair out of his eyes, a good reminder that he was beginning to appear a bit shaggy. That wouldn't do. Not if he meant to look like a proper steward and not some wandering gypsy.

Once the chill of the water began to settle beneath his skin he made for the small clump of rocks where he'd left his clothes. As he found his footing he looked up – to see a pair of large green eyes with slits for pupils gazing back at him. He stopped, not because he didn't know a cat's eyes when he saw them, but because they seemed to be floating several feet above the ground. That required an immediate and logical explanation.

"You seem to enjoy the lake," Isabel's voice came. The cat's eyes shifted a little, and then he could make out the woman's silhouette standing just back from the shoreline, the feline in her arms.

"I decided it would be simpler than a bath," he returned.

"I imagine so. We're about to sit for dinner, if you'd care to join us."

Until that second it hadn't occurred to him that he needed an invitation. *Damnation.* She wasn't a cousin, and this estate didn't belong to one of his relations. There were rules, and he needed to keep in mind which of them applied to him now. "'Us' meaning you and Miss Jane, I assume?"

"Of course."

"Thank you. I would be pleased to join you."

She continued to gaze at him, her eyes, unlike the cat's green reflecting orbs, shadowed in the deepening night. "Are you coming, then?" she finally asked.

Adam cleared his throat. "If you wouldn't mind turning your back. I'm a bit...naked."

"Oh! Oh."

He couldn't see her blush in the dark, but he could imagine her doing so. Then again, she hadn't thought twice about seeking out the half-naked figures carved into the dining room fireplace. Nevertheless, she and the cat shifted, one of the green discs disappearing. Well, he would have to assume that only the cat was looking. There wouldn't be much to see in the dark, anyway.

Adam scowled as he splashed out of the water. Of course there was much – a great deal – to see, but it *was* getting quite dark, and the water was cold. He took a breath. He was being an idiot. Thank God he was keeping his commentary to himself. Putting his bare backside on one of the rocks, he toweled himself off with his shirt, then pulled on his trousers and his boots. The rest would have to wait, and he needed something nicer for dinner, anyway.

"Where did the cat come from?" he asked, standing to stomp into his second boot.

"I don't know. I went into my bedchamber to change for dinner and it was sitting on the bed. Simmons said he 'wasn't aware the house had a resident feline." She imitated the butler's slightly nasal tone as she spoke.

"You have a talent for mimicry," he noted, grinning.

"Do I?" She sighed audibly. "It's not at all proper, I'm sure."

"As you just caught me out swimming naked, your secret is safe with me, Isabel." He liked saying her name aloud even more than he'd liked repeating it in his mind. Moving up beside her, he offered his hand. "It can be slippery at the water's edge."

She gripped his fingers with her free hand, and they made their way back toward the path. Her skin felt warm and soft against his rough palms, and he resisted the urge to tighten his hold. He was rendering assistance; that was all.

"You seem to have forgotten half your clothes," she noted, as they left the thickest growth of trees and shrubbery behind.

He could practically feel her gaze. Warmth trailed pleasantly through him. "My shirt's sweaty," he said, hefting it. "My waistcoat and jacket are behind the house. I need to change for dinner, anyway."

"I'm not complaining," she returned, leaving him to wonder whether she was being practical or flirtatious. He hoped it was the latter.

As they reached the path, lit by widely spaced torches and consisting of well-compacted earth and scattered, rounded pebbles, Adam released her fingers before she could remember that it wasn't proper for them to be hand in hand. If there was one thing he wanted, it was for her never to have to feel wary of him, or worried that he wouldn't conduct himself like a gentleman. She was an unmarried young lady, and she needed his assistance. That had to come first. Even if other thoughts had been pushing at the back of his mind since he'd set eyes on her.

"You should give your horse a name," she said in the silence filled by frogs and cricket songs.

That hadn't been at all where his thoughts were headed, and he wrenched them back around. "I've no objection to that. Perhaps you should name him, though."

"Well, what would *you* call him?"

Adam shrugged. "Boy? Red? Chestnut? Horse?"

"Oh, dear. What about King? Or Major?"

"Major will do," he returned. "Major it is, th—"

"Or Flame? Ember? Oh, Copper."

"Copper's splendi—"

"No, no. Let me think."

He walked beside her, more amused than he could remember being for quite a long time. Her mind was like a firefly, bright and flitting from one thought to the next, quick and warm. It wasn't that she couldn't decide, he realized. She was genuinely searching for the best fit. "You're next, you know," he mouthed at the cat. It blinked at him.

"You said he's steady and well-behaved, yes?"

"Yes."

"Firefly, then, to give him some spirit."

Adam blinked. Yes, he'd been thinking about fireflies, but he hadn't said anything aloud. It had to be a coincidence, of course. "I—"

"No. You're a man. One of you might be teased for a little name like Firefly. I wouldn't want his feelings hurt."

He'd rather lost hold of the reins at this point. Best simply go along for the ride, then. "Of course not."

"Abel, then. No, he was the brother who got murdered in the Bible." She glanced up, her footsteps slowing. "Oh, my. Orion?"

He followed her gaze. The stars had begun blinking into sight, one after the other, until the sky looked nearly cloudy with them. He loved clear nights like this. They were few and far between. "I like Orion," he said into the quiet.

"Then you should call him Orion."

Adam nodded, smiling at her. "I will. Thank you, from me and from Orion."

Isabel grinned back at him. "You're welcome. It's a good name, I think."

"Did you find that orb you were after?" he pursued, abruptly wishing the path back to the house had a few more twists and turns.

Her shoulders rose and fell. "No. I feel like I should know where it is, and I've given in and asked everyone now, but Simmons doesn't think it's been seen in nearly twenty years."

"Forgive me for stating the obvious, but might your mother have taken it with her when she left for Italy?"

"No. That would have been impossible."

He didn't see a family heirloom leaving with a family member as even close to impossible, but she did sound very certain. "The attic, perhaps?"

"I took a quick look, but the attic is quite large. It could be there. I'm beginning to think it might not be meant for me, though."

"And why is that? You said it's been in your family for ages. That does include you."

She sent him a sideways smile. "I would explain it, but I know for a fact that it all sounds a bit mad." Isabel hefted the small gray tabby in her arms. "Before you replace those railings on the garden steps, would you help me sketch out a plan for an orangery overlooking the garden? We had oranges in Florence, and I always loved the scent of them, but I've heard it snows here in winter."

"It can." Adam nodded, his mind already seizing on her suggestion and spinning it about with square footage and the current price of glass for the many windows that would be required. The addition would take up the area he was presently digging up for the replacement steps and railings, but it was doable.

It would have been more convenient if she'd mentioned an orangery before he'd placed the order for new railings, but he doubted the smith had begun yet. And building an orangery could certainly provide more than enough work for the man to make up for the cancelled order. And it could provide Adam with another chance to do something well and correctly the first time – a feat that continued to elude him at Nimway Hall.

"I know that seems abrupt and ill-considered, for me to arrive one day and the next suggest major construction," she went on, apparently misreading his silence, "but I thought it better to look into it now rather than after you put the replacement railing in."

"I appreciate your timing, actually," he countered. "And considering your new bee apiary, orange trees and orange blossom honey could well be the grandest idea of the year."

"Oh, we could sell Nimway honey at the market. I loved the fresh orange honey back in Florence." She put her fingers to her chin. "We'll need more chests of drawers to grow our hive." Isabel grinned.

He liked her smile. Very much. Laughing, he tried to focus his attention on something other than kissing her curved, soft-looking lips. "A fitting emblem, at the least."

"Yes, we could call it Top-Drawer Honey." She chuckled. "We must do it, now."

They reached the foot of the half-dismantled steps, and Adam collected his remaining clothes before he again offered his hand to help steady her. At the door, he released her once more. "Please don't wait dinner for me. I'll be down in just a moment."

He carried thoughts of her with him as he retreated up the back stairs. Could an estate steward, an employee, pursue the mistress of a grand house? It seemed possible. Her own mother had married a sculptor, after all. And he *was* well-born, even if he'd chosen not to pursue a career in the army or the clergy.

Adam paused outside his bedchamber door. The fact remained that he did work for her, and that by necessity they had to live beneath the same roof. If he acted and she rebuffed him, he could lose both Nimway and any chance at...more than a friendship with her. Though if someone of Alton's ilk had been his employer, even a friendship between owner and employee would neither be looked for nor expected.

In a single day Isabel de Rossi had turned a quiet, waiting household into an unexpected, interesting one. He liked it, actually, and more than he would have thought. In his experience an estate required order and discipline, and around her he felt neither composed nor logical. And yet he couldn't deny that over the last day he felt more...alive. If that was the trade-off, he welcomed it.

Would simply being here be enough for him, though? Could he watch while other men courted her and one of them won her hand? And was he being a fool for even wondering where he might fit now in this very changeable place?

CHAPTER 7

"I'm not naming her Miss or Mrs. anything," Isabel stated, rolling a ball of yarn across her bed. The small gray cat looked at it approaching, then set one paw atop the knotted green orb, stopping its advance. "I detest my grandmother's cat, Miss Tatterbell. She glared at me disapprovingly for the entire fortnight we were in London."

"Perhaps she already has a name," Jane suggested, standing beside the bed to pin up the last, escaping strands of Isabel's dark hair. "She didn't just appear out of a cloud of mist. She's young, but she wasn't born yesterday. And to be as tame as she is, she must belong to someone."

"I've asked. No one can recall ever seeing her before yesterday. They have an orange cat in the stable, but Billy hasn't seen this one before, either." As she watched, the striped gray cat sat up straight, the end of her tail flicking restlessly. "Mist. That's a splendid suggestion, Jane."

"I thought for certain you'd go directly to Guinevere or some other legendary female."

Isabel wrinkled her nose. "Perhaps if I were eight years old." Even so, the name did appeal to her. It just seemed very…on the nose. If the legends were true, she *was* a descendant of Merlin and Nimue, after all. It was easy to be convinced of a truth when one lived half a continent away from where it resided. She leaned down to rest her chin on her fists, eye-to-eye with the mysterious feline. "Do you like Mist?"

The cat stood, padding forward to bump her nose against Isabel's before she jumped down from the bed and made her way to the door.

"That looked like agreement to me," Jane conceded. "And she is quite lovely, all gray tabby stripes and those big green eyes."

"She is a beauty, isn't she? I'll give her up if someone comes to claim her, but in the meantime, she's Mist."

Isabel stood as well, made a quick check of her appearance in the dressing mirror, and opened the bedchamber door for the cat. Well, she'd had no luck finding the famous orb, but she had discovered a kitty. And Adam hadn't scoffed at her idea for an orangery. In fact, he'd seemed to think it rather brilliant. All in all, a good place to be on her third day at Nimway Hall.

Downstairs she selected her breakfast from the sideboard and sat at the table to eat. Mist the cat found a sunny spot beneath one of the windows and curled into a gray striped ball – which Simmons stepped over with exaggerated care to present her with a silver platter.

"A missive arrived for you earlier this morning, Miss Isabel," he said, lowering the salver with great ceremony so she could pluck the folded piece of paper from it. "And Mr. Driscoll awaits your convenience in the garden."

"Thank you, Simmons."

With a curious glance at Jane seated across from her, Isabel broke the wax seal, some sort of flower and a fish, and unfolded the letter. "It's from Lord Alton," she said, dropping her gaze immediately to the signature at the bottom.

"The viscount from yesterday?" her companion asked. "You must have made an impression."

"Please, Jane."

"Well, you said he was handsome."

And so he was. Also very self-assured, especially in comparison to her. She shifted her attention to the top of the letter. "Dear Isabel," she read to herself, "I am writing this immediately upon my return to Blackbridge. Indeed, the words I mean to put down have dogged me for the entire duration of my ride. I—"

"What does he say?" Jane asked.

"I don't know yet. He's still talking about when he wrote it. Hush." Isabel settled in again. "I knew you to be a young lady, but I had no idea you would be a reincarnation of the goddess Aphrodite." She stopped, looking up again. "He says I'm Aphrodite," she reported.

"That's a fine beginning, then."

Yes, it was. Fine and flattering. And just so perfect she had to force herself to be at least a little skeptical. "It could also mean he thinks to flatter me because he wants something."

Jane lifted an eyebrow. "Of course he wants something. Your hand in marriage."

"If that's so, he'll have to spend more than three hours in my company," Isabel noted. There. That sounded very practical. "And half of those were him distracting me while I tried to listen to Adam and the blacksmith."

"You're just teasing me. I know you liked him." Her companion waved a hand at the missive. "Go on, now."

"I'll just read the rest of it aloud, then, shall I?"

"Yes, please."

Stifling a smile, Isabel cleared her throat. "'In my sudden, overwhelmed admiration, I fear I stepped too far,'" she read, noting that Simmons had ceased even the pretense of straightening things in favor of baldly listening. "'Of course I could not expect you to join me for luncheon without first giving you the opportunity to discover my character and reputation from those around you whom you trust.'"

"Very sensible," Jane said approvingly.

"Yes, well, I thought the overstepping to which he referred

would be when he suggested I replace my steward with someone of his choosing." He'd actually inferred someone more *competent*, but Isabel wasn't about to say any such thing in front of the servants.

"Well, he's more concerned about how you feel toward him, which is understandable."

"Are you trying to convince me to swoon for the first man to say hello? Because he needs more to recommend him than having the prime place in the queue of gentlemen callers." She was a woman of property, after all. Everyone had warned her she would have men at her front door. It just so happened that the first one to appear was very easy on the eyes.

"Keep reading, then."

"Fine. 'In the hope that you will have done so and that you approve of my character, I will be in East Pennard for market day on Monday next. If you would join me to walk among the stalls, I will be most pleased, and will consider that my initial misstep has been forgiven. If I receive less – a nod, or nothing at all – on that day, it will be enough for me to know that you cannot forgive me, and we'll speak no more of possibilities. Yours in hope, Alton.'"

Jane slapped her hand against the tabletop. "Now *that* is a true gentleman. And a romantic."

It *did* sound very sincere. And a suggestion of possibilities that seemed much less...confining than what she'd felt from him yesterday relieved her greatly. "In retrospect, the suggestion of a luncheon doesn't seem so very unforgivable," she said aloud.

"Indeed."

"If...If he passes muster with those here who know of him. Simmons?"

The butler cleared his throat, straightening from the sideboard. "I...Ah, I cannot speak of my betters, Miss Isabel."

"Of course you can. What do you know of Geoffrey Spratt-Bell, Viscount Alton?"

"If you insist, Miss Isabel. From what I've heard first- and second-hand Lord Alton keeps a neat house, divides his time between here and Alton Park in Wells, was once betrothed to a young lady who died of...influenza, I believe, and is generally well-respected by his tenants and staff."

"Well, that was very concise," Jane said, putting her hand over her smile.

"Indeed, it was," Isabel seconded. "Do you have a paragraph ready for all the local gentry?"

"If I did not know your neighbors, their politics, and their culinary likes and dislikes, I would not be a very efficient butler," the butler returned, lifting an eyebrow. "I could even tell you that he takes a splash of milk and two sugars in his tea, but I believe that knowledge is only of import to the footmen, should Lord Alton come calling."

"I am most impressed, Simmons."

He inclined his head grandly. "Miss Isabel."

It seemed she was going to market on Monday next. Isabel finished her breakfast, her heart much lighter than it had been yesterday, and went off to find Adam.

He wore a shirt and waistcoat this morning, which disappointed her a little. She was the daughter of a famous sculptor, after all – it might not be proper, but she couldn't help noticing a fine, well-muscled chest and back when she saw them. And Adam Driscoll was a very fine-looking man.

Last night walking beside him beneath the stars had been, well, very close to magical. And he'd held her hand twice, assisting her over the rough ground. It had been well after dinner before her mind seized onto reason again enough to remind her firstly that he worked for her, and secondly that he wasn't the sort of man he'd imagined for herself. A polished, proper husband, someone whose strengths lay in her weaknesses, would be much more beneficial to her standing and reputation with her neighbors – and in London.

Aside from that, while he'd sent her a few looks subject to interpretation, he'd only touched her when strictly necessary for her safety. He treated her very properly, in fact – warm and friendly but also professional and competent. And that was how it should be.

Adam would remain for as long as she needed him, and then she would send him away with a very positive letter of recommendation. And whatever she might momentarily dream about his calloused, capable hands or his rare, infectious smile, that was for her to reconcile.

"You wanted to see me?" she asked, before anyone could accuse her of staring. She stopped above the half-ruined back steps above him.

He looked up, the furrow between his brows smoothing as he met her gaze. "Yes. Might we sit down somewhere and discuss what you want in an orangery? With your permission I thought to write up your ideas and my notations on size and location and send them to an architect of my acquaintance in Glastonbury. Or I could deliver them to him myself – unless you had someone in mind."

"Perhaps we could both go meet this architect, or invite him here. Whatever we decide must match the architecture of the Hall."

He nodded, easily hopping over a pile of rubble as he made his way up to her through the debris. "Yes. A good idea, to have him come here. Nimway Hall is unique and tends to defy description. Without seeing it himself, I doubt he could match its charming, timeless quality."

Abruptly she was glad she'd thought of the orangery now, rather than after she sent him away. It wasn't about extending his employment and keeping him about, of course; while she learned how to be a steward – a guardian – herself, his appreciation for the house and his thoughtfulness about preserving its qualities could only help her do the same later, on her own.

"The music room?" she suggested. "We can see the steps from there, as well as the lake. All we need is a table beneath the windows."

"Excellent. Shall we divide and conquer? Give me a few

minutes to direct the lads about where we're moving the rubble, and I'll join you there."

"I'll see to the table, then." And she liked that he'd assumed she could manage a task, even if it was a terribly simple one. Did he know, then, that she meant to take over his position? If he did, it didn't seem to trouble him – or he was too polite to show any resentment. She hoped it was the former. And she hoped he did realize this wouldn't last forever, because she didn't want to see the surprise on his face when she had to tell him.

FOR TWO HOURS they sat in the old music room, table and two chairs as close to the windows as they could manage. Isabel claimed to have inherited none of her father's artistic talent, but as Adam watched her sketch delicate wrought-iron filigrees for the doors and windows, he decided she was either unaware of her own skill, or she was being too modest. Given her forthright manner of speaking, he tended to favor the former.

"Is it too much?" she asked, wrinkling her nose at the latest sketch. "I don't want anyone pointing at it and thinking, 'Well, someone's full of themselves'."

Adam chuckled. "It matches the scrolling on the fireplace, which matches the filigree on the wainscoting. It links the house together."

She blew out her breath. "Oh, good. I did want to give some additional work to Mr. Coopering, since I pulled the iron railing order out from under him."

God, she was perfect. Blinking that abrupt thought away, he took the sketch to make a few more notes about scale and quantity. "With your permission I'll write Mr. Hodgins the architect and invite him to come out on Monday. You'll likely be expected to lodge him while he draws up the plans, if that's acceptable."

A muscle in her cheek twitched. "Tuesday would be better. I'd like to see the East Pennard market on Monday."

How had he managed to forget the market? *Idiot.* "Of course. The market will give you a good sense of your community, I think, and I can introduce you to whomever you haven't met by then."

Her cheeks reddened. "Actually, Lord Alton has already offered to escort me, and I've accepted."

"Ah." Adam clenched his jaw and decided a few more notations were necessary.

"What does that mean?"

"What does what mean?"

"'Ah'. If you have a specific complaint about the viscount I would like to know it. The two of you clearly share some sort of animosity."

That transparent, was he? "As a gentleman, I have no answer to give you," he returned.

She glared at him, clearly exasperated. "You're generally more forthcoming than this, Adam. Has he done you an ill turn?"

As much as he wanted to declare that Alton's ill turn was an unforgiveable sin, that had always been a matter of philosophical and moral interpretation. And stating that in general he disliked the man because Bell-Spratt viewed no one with as much care or affection as he did himself, smacked of smallness.

Adam liked Isabel, but he couldn't precisely claim the high ground in a battle of propriety firstly when he had nothing to offer a woman of wealth and property, and secondly when using his position in her household had begun to appeal to him. "That is a matter of some debate. He and I would give you opposing answers, and no doubt each of us believes he is in the right."

When Isabel reached over to grasp his hand, he flinched. "I don't know you well, Adam Driscoll, but you do seem an honorable man with a great measure of common sense. Is there something about Lord Alton that troubles you? Surely you have a reason for your dislike."

Reasoning out what he wanted to say, Adam slowly looked up to meet her stormy gray eyes. Three days, and he was already lost at sea, drowning in the depths of that warm, clever gaze. Honor demanded that he hold onto the shore, and he gripped the shifting sand with all his might. "I do have a reason. But he may have changed. He seems to admire you, which is a point in his favor. His... The way he views life and those who cross his path doesn't match well with my own views. You may not find that to be so."

She studied his face for several hard beats of his heart, while he held himself back from the mad desire to lean across the table and kiss her. He very nearly broke before she abruptly released his hand.

"I believe you to be an honest and true gentleman," she said quietly, and patted the back of his hand as if he were her doting grandfather. "And I hope you will always be so honest with me."

Obviously she saw this as a great compliment, an oath of sorts to be given and received seriously. An honor. And he *was* honored that she trusted him. Being relegated to eternal friendship, though, was another matter entirely, and one he didn't like. At all. Even so, he nodded. "I will always speak the truth to you," he said aloud.

There were merely some things he wouldn't speak of at all.

THE NEXT TWO days flew by, with Adam showing Isabel her property and introducing her to every servant, worker, and tenant they could fit into the day. And considering that everyone they met had to share a meal or a drink or at the least a story about their ancestors and hers, the days filled quickly. It slowed them down massively, but the introductions clearly delighted both her and the residents surrounding Nimway Hall. As he listened to each tale, he began to understand how deeply the connection between these tenants and the succession of women in Isabel's bloodline truly went.

For a hundred years, two hundred, perhaps a thousand years, Nimway Hall in one form or another had stood, and a woman had been present as caretaker and guardian. And according to nearly everyone, that female was the reason the land had flourished. Some of the stories were so ancient they fell into the realm of myth – and it was in those he first heard about the connection between this place and Merlin, along with his so-called Lady of the Lake. Of all the things Adam might have expected to learn about Isabel de Rossi, a connection to a fairy tale hadn't been one of them.

"So the legends have you as a direct descendant of Merlin and the witch Nimue," he commented, carefully steering the wagon they'd had to borrow up the steep, switch-backed path climbing the escarpment. Orion and Fiore were tied at the rear, the former doing his best to reach the baskets of vegetables that sat among the other gifts from the farmers and villagers.

Isabel kept her gaze on the widening view of the valley below them. "We should use all this for a feast. They've given me far too much, but I didn't know how to refuse without seeming rude or haughty. Could we host a luncheon in the next week, do you think? Or a breakfast?"

"With some time to get canopies and extra tables and chairs from Glastonbury, we could. Give me a day or so, but they'll all need to know as soon as possible." He considered it. "A luncheon after church might be best; everyone should be free to attend."

"Let's do that, then. Thank you."

"You're welcome. But do you intend to let them go on thinking you're related to myths? That might have been believable two or three hundred years ago, but this is the nineteenth century."

"I *am* related to them. Nimue's hut was here, where the house stands now. The stories are old, but that doesn't make them false."

"You actually believe that?" She seemed so practical, and well-read, and intelligent. Perhaps he shouldn't have asked that question aloud, but Merlin and *magic*? The world wasn't magic.

"You say that like you think I shouldn't believe it," she said, facing him. "The house, the property, is named after her. The spelling's changed over the years, but it's the same Nimway. And Merlin was her love."

"And the Giant's Causeway in Ireland and Scotland was made by the giant Fionn mac Cumhaill tossing rocks into the sea," he retorted.

"That's a tale to explain the odd shaped stones," she said, her eyes narrowing. "And while I've never seen a giant, I've never seen stones elsewhere that look like those, either."

"Then you believe in giants *and* Merlin?"

"And you don't?"

"I believe ignorant people make up stories to explain things they cannot make sense of. I do not believe that a wizard can wave his hands in the air and cause one man to take on the face of another, or snap his fingers to light a candle unless he's secretly holding flints in his fingers."

Even as he spoke, he had the feeling that he'd just stumbled into a bog, and that no matter which way he turned or what he said next, he was about to fall in over his head. At the same time, how else was he supposed to react? Going along with this nonsense would be an insult to both of them.

Her lips tightened. "So you think me an ignorant fool," she said flatly.

And the mud closed in around him. "I don't think you either. I've seen evidence to the contrary."

"A silly child, then."

"Naïve, perhaps," he hedged. "If you grew up with such tales, of course you must have believed them as a young girl."

"I see."

What the devil could he say to ease her frown? Because it abruptly seemed very important that he do so. "Isabel, y—"

"I do *not* believe in fire-breathing dragons," she cut in sharply. "I *do* believe there is more in this world than what you see around you at this moment in time. I've never seen the wind twisting into a funnel all the way up to the sky, but I believe the people who say they've seen such a thing. And where would you find evidence for that?"

"Wind storms and magic are two different things."

"You believe as you wish. I shall do the same."

"Th—"

She lifted a hand. "No. I am finished with this discussion. And before you say that you pity my ignorance, I pity that you can't believe just a little bit of magic exists in the world." With that, she folded her arms across her chest and turned as far away from him as she could on the narrow wooden seat.

Adam clenched his jaw. She'd asked him to speak the truth, and he'd done so. It was hardly his fault that she didn't like what he'd said. At the same time, an employee arguing with an employer as he had would, in any other circumstances, likely become unemployed at this point.

But he wondered how Lord Alton would respond if she told *him* she was a descendant of Merlin and Nimue. If it would help the viscount secure her extremely lucrative timber rights, he would more than likely humor her. Of course growing up in the area, handsome Geoffrey probably knew the legends already.

Which left him, an outsider no one had bothered to tell, so that he had no option but to be surprised when she broadsided him with it. Adam drew in a hard breath. Yes, the legend had surprised him; her *belief* in the legend had stunned him.

Should he have lied about that? Should he have smiled and said that of course he believed in magic? How else could one explain rainbows and cyclonic winds? And what was he supposed to do now – show her tricks and then explain them away with logic and science? Just accept that a woman of eighteen years – his employer – believed in magic?

He supposed he would have to do just that if he wanted to remain at Nimway Hall, which he did. She didn't seem likely to change her mind, and he damned well wouldn't change his.

CHAPTER 8

"*W*ell, what would you have thought of him, truly, if he'd said he saw fairies in the garden and pigs that flew themselves to market?"

Isabel frowned at Jane, missing a step and nearly tripping over a basket of straw dolls. "I would have thought he was mocking me, just as you are."

Jane's generally affable expression drew into a scowl of her own. "Miss Isabel, I've known you since you were one year old, when your mama decided you should have an English nanny. I read all those books to you. I played evil knights and brave princesses with you. I have never, and I will never, mock you."

Sometimes Isabel still felt like that little girl, thinking before she'd thought it through, letting her own feelings dictate how she reacted to others. "I apologize, Jane. You have been a staunch ally since before I can remember. That stupid man has had me tilting at windmills for three days. Everything I hear is an insult, and I must defend myself."

"Adam Driscoll has never seen magic, Isabel. Truth be told, have you? Perhaps he only requires some patience. And some proof."

Isabel opened her mouth to reply that of course she'd seen magic – Jane had slept through that glorious first sunrise at Nimway Hall, but that hadn't been *her* fault. And that had been magical. But if she mentioned it, her companion would want to know what she considered the difference between *magic* and *magical*, and they would both end in foul moods. "You've heard about the orb and my parents, just as I have," she said instead. "And so many other things."

"Yes, I have. And I've seen you spend hours digging through every room and the attic looking for that orb, without success. It might have been a metaphor, you know."

"You've seen the birthmark behind my left shoulder. *That* is the orb. It's not a meta—"

"Just please keep in mind, my dove, that a very few years ago here in England they believed enough in magic to burn witches. And now they toss old ladies into Bedlam for saying their cats talk to them. Neither sounds particularly appealing."

"Now I'm a potential Bedlamite. Wonderful. Well, for your information, Mist has yet to speak to me."

It felt easier as they walked through the crowded market to make Jane's warning into a half-offended jest. She knew full well what her companion meant, though – that perhaps it wasn't Adam Driscoll who'd been unreasonable last Friday.

She'd barely spoken to him since then, and only when strictly necessary. Despite that, their luncheon in the meadow had been a spectacular success, and her head still spun from meeting so many people. People for whose well-being she was now responsible, and who'd been so pleased to have her there despite the fact that she now had a very good grasp on the fact that Nimway worked on a much grander scale than anything she'd previously experienced.

That had made her sleep restless for the past few nights, and after the picnic yesterday she hadn't slept at all. It was also the reason she hadn't changed her mind yet again about Mr. Driscoll and sent him packing. Still, the more quickly she learned his job and how he went about it, the sooner she could part ways with this man whose imagination seemed firmly stuck in the mud. And whomever she hired to replace him would not be as blasted stubborn.

"I believe that is your beau coming this way, Isabel," Jane whispered, wrenching her out of her mental morass. "If you keep frowning like that, you'll send him fleeing."

"He's not my beau," she returned, sending a smile in Lord Alton's direction as the viscount approached, a single yellow rose in one hand. *Not yet, anyway.* But his odds had certainly improved once she'd heard the unsatisfactory philosophy of her unsuitable steward. And that was just as well.

"Good morning, Isabel," he greeted her, sweeping a bow and at the same time taking hold of her fingers to kiss her knuckles. "I am not skilled in the language of flowers, but my gardener informs me that yellow roses signify sorrow or regret. I then decided that must also include apologies, though I could be completely wrong. I make no guarantees." With that he held the rose out to her.

Isabel laughed, curtsying as she took the flower. At least someone had a sense of humor. No wonder Adam didn't like him. "Thank you, my lord. And please do stop apologizing. The affront was slight, at best."

His smile deepening, he moved around beside her to offer his arm. "Then let me show you a very fine example of a village market."

"Please do."

With Jane trailing behind them, they wandered among the wagons and boxes and blankets and more elaborate stalls, accepting samples of strawberries and other fresh flowers, spending pennies and shillings on delicate seed- and shell-bracelets, a variety of jams and preserves, and a pair of pretty knitted gloves. At every stall they had to stop and chat, met by eager farmers and craftsmen who'd lived their lives on land she owned. She received still more invitations to visit, questions about livestock the answers for which she had to defer to Lord

Alton, and one complaint about a neighbor's sheep dog scaring cows and putting them off milk for a week.

"They adore you already," Geoffrey noted, as she finished promising to speak to the dog's owner. "They've missed having a guardian here since your grandmother left."

Her heart thudding, she looked up at him. "You know about the guardians of Nimway Hall?"

"I grew up ten miles from here. I daresay all your neighbors have cast jealous gazes at your fertile fields and thick wood and asked how and why, that despite the fact that we already know the answer: the land was long ago blessed by Merlin and the Lady Nimue, and their descendants continue their legacy."

"And do you believe that?" she asked, carefully keeping her expression neutral. This line of questioning hadn't gone at all well when she'd attempted it with Adam.

The viscount chuckled. "'There are more things in heaven and earth, Horatio, than are dreamt of in your philosophy,'" he said, snagging an orange and tossing it into the air to catch it again.

"Precisely! The worst a naysayer can claim is that they haven't personally witnessed anything."

His gaze on her, he abruptly flashed her another smile. "I have no proof the tales aren't true, and it's ungentlemanly to disparage a lady's ancestry. There are a plenitude of tales surrounding Glastonbury and King Arthur. And how do you explain Stonehenge without bringing magic and Merlin into the equation?"

"Thank you for saying that." And thank goodness someone else felt as she did. She only wished stuffy Mr. Driscoll had been there to overhear. And she wished she'd thought of the example of Stonehenge. She would certainly bring it up to him the next time they spoke – if they spoke.

Alton inclined his head. "Ask any of your tenants, Isabel. They know precisely who you are, and from whom you're descended."

Nearly everyone she'd met had certainly made their respect for her clear enough, whether she'd done anything to earn that or not. Some of them had seemed almost...overcome at seeing her.

She'd put that to them being without a landlord for so long then suddenly having one knocking on the door, but it had been eye-opening. People *needed* her, and for some reason she hadn't expected that. "May I ask you something, Geoffrey?"

"Of course."

"Does all this become...routine? The—" She stopped as a young girl curtsied and handed her a fistful of cornflowers. "Thank you, my sweet," she said, smiling and bringing the flowers to her nose. "These are lovely."

Blushing, the girl pranced off to rejoin her parents at their stall, which boasted loaves of delightful-smelling fresh bread. Isabel immediately signaled Jane to purchase two loaves for breakfast tomorrow.

"Routine, yes," the viscount responded, once they'd passed by the stall. "I can't tell you how many pretty rocks or flowers my steward or I've received, all in hopes one of us will be charmed enough to pay for repairing a roof or purchasing a new milk cow to replace the dried-up one the poor family will have to eat if I cruelly turn them down."

She chuckled at his dramatics. "I'm pleased I enjoy pretty rocks, then."

"Oh, you've no idea. One farmer claimed that because my grandfather had given his grandfather a pair of pigs, I was there-fore responsible for replacing a sow because, and I quote, 'the pigs is used to being a pair'. As if I was the one to let the thing out to eat rabbit droppings or whatever it got into."

He wasn't jesting. As that realization struck her, Isabel could only hope her mouth wasn't agape. "That seems rather cynical," she said slowly. "You do help your tenants, do you not? Who else would they turn to?"

One of his arched brows dipped. "Oh." Geoffrey gave a forced-sounding laugh. "I was only jesting, Isabel. There's no need to be distressed. Each household has an agreement with me, some of them made generations ago. Within each agreement has been laid out the rent the tenant pays, either in blunt or in goods produced, and what repairs, support, etcetera, the landlord is obligated to supply. I always fulfill my end of that bargain. Flowers and tea cakes and claims of broken pig hearts aren't necessary."

Did she have such contracts and agreements? If so, where were they? She would have to ask Adam, blast it all. But at least it explained Alton's position in regard to his tenants. With two properties, he likely had far more people for whom he was responsible than she did. That explained why he held to the agreements so closely. It still felt...too by the book, as if she could decide not to help a farmer purchase a badly needed new cow or pig because a centuries-old piece of paper said she didn't have any legal duty to do so.

It seemed cold-hearted and his jest – if that was what it had been – rather sharp-edged, but she didn't know enough about any of this to pronounce judgment. Especially against someone with far more experience than she had. Adam, at least, seemed to think she lacked a certain mental discipline, and perhaps in this he was correct.

"Of course I couldn't resist bringing you a flower, either, so who am I to say?" Alton commented into the silence, his easy smile reappearing.

For goodness's sake he was charming. Far more so than her rude steward. "I've been thinking," she said. "Perhaps meeting you for luncheon wasn't such a poor idea, after all."

"You are a very wise young lady," he returned. "We missed our chance last Wednesday, but perhaps the one two days from hence will suffice?"

"I believe it will."

~

ADAM LEANED against the flimsy wall of a stall, arms crossed over his chest and his half-lidded gaze on the couple halfway across the market square. He couldn't hear what they said, but he damned well recognized the frequent smiles and hands touching and the idiotic yellow rose.

Three older brothers kept him from inheriting his father's barony, but he was still a damned aristocrat. He wasn't a viscount, certainly, and apparently unforgivably he worked with his hands and had very little in the way of money. Or perhaps more unfortunately, he'd spoken his mind to his employer.

"I can make you a smaller one, if you'd like," came from beside him.

Shaking himself, Adam straightened. "That's not necessary, Hayward. Miss Isabel would like to begin a proper apiary. I think two hives to begin with. And we know these bees like living in square things."

The old farmer snorted. "I did hear about that. A mahogany chest of drawers, they say, once owned by Henry the Eighth. Now it's got bee shit and honey all over it."

So now it was old Henry. A few days ago it had only been George the Third. The chest was getting older and more valuable by the day, despite the obvious neglect to which they were subjecting it. And *that* was how tales began. If he and Isabel ever spoke again, he would use her beehive as an example. "I'll throw in an extra quid if you'll help me move the bees out of the chest and into the hives."

The farmer grinned. "For a quid I'll do it myself, Mr. Driscoll."

Adam stuck out his hand. "That is a deal."

He and the farmer shook on it, and Hayward agreed to have the box hives ready by Friday. It would have been just as easy to send to London for them, but Adam would only have done that as a last resort. Anything that helped grow the local economy would help Nimway thrive, and Hayward's own hives were legendary for the quality of their honey.

The luncheon yesterday had left the house short of butter and salt and a few other kitchen basics, so he wasn't surprised to see Mrs. Dall, the cook, a few stalls away making purchases for the household. He should have thought of holding a gathering on

Isabel's behalf, but considering how well it had gone he was glad the idea had been hers. Despite his frustration with her, her openness and easy friendship spoke well for the future of the property. Her tenants were only just beginning to feel comfortable enough to speak honestly with him, and over the course of one luncheon she'd done what it had taken him weeks to accomplish.

He, of course, would have to remember that her request for honesty from him didn't include his views on magic. From what he could see of Isabel and Alton this morning, she either hadn't brought up the fact that she believed a ball could vanish from one hand and appear in the other, or she had done so – and the viscount had then quoted *Hamlet* about there being more things than man could explain. Never mind that *Hamlet* was at its heart a well-spoken ghost story. Of course it would have supernatural elements in it. That didn't make it true.

"Was there something more you wanted, Mr. Driscoll?" Hayward asked. "God knows I'm happy to have you spend your money here."

Adam pulled himself back to the market once more. "Hmm? No. Sorry, I was just lost in a daydream."

"She's pretty enough to send even an old man like me dreaming," the farmer noted, following Adam's gaze.

Damnation. "I wasn't—"

"If she's heard the orb speak Lord Alton's name, lad, you'll have to settle for your daydreams."

Orb? The same orb for which Isabel had been searching? "There's another shilling in it for you if you tell me what this orb is, Hayward."

"I ain't ever set eyes on it, but I've heard it's old. Older than time, maybe. Some say it's a crystal. Some say it was the capstone of Merlin's very staff. Old Widow May swears it's part of a giant's crown."

Magic again, of course. That explanation hardly seemed worth a shilling since he'd heard much the same thing at the picnic yesterday, but he'd given his word. Digging into a pocket, he produced a coin and set it into the chuckling Hayward's palm.

"Anything else you want to know, you come see me." The farmer walked forward to greet another visitor to his stall. "And don't you worry, Mr. Driscoll. I'll deliver those hives to you myself come Friday."

Adam nodded, mentally crossing his fingers that he'd run through the ill luck where the bees were concerned. If he wanted to keep his job he couldn't afford another fiasco. Especially now. As quickly as he could, keeping well away from Isabel and her escort mostly so he wouldn't be tempted – more tempted – to punch the viscount, he met with the other people he needed to see this morning.

That finished, he sent the laughing pair a last, annoyed glare, then reclaimed Orion and headed back toward the escarpment and the house beyond. He, at least, had work to do today. Even as that petty thought crossed his mind, though, he admitted it wasn't fair. Yes, she had a great deal to learn about Nimway Hall, its occupants, and which bits of it required the most careful attention. She also needed to become acquainted with the entire rhythm of the place, with its quirks and its characters, and thus far she'd very nearly outstripped him in that regard. And being in the market square today was part of that. The company she kept there didn't matter.

Stephens and his son, young Stephens, were already clearing the last of the rubble from the front of the garden, so Adam trotted up the stairs to his bedchamber to change into his work clothes. Even at a minimum size the orangery would entail moving a dozen bushes and a flower bed in addition to the warped steps and railing, and he wanted it all finished before Mr. Hodgins arrived tomorrow.

As he pulled on his work gloves a gray shadow startled him, darting from beneath the bed and jumping onto the windowsill. "You need a collar with a bell on it, Mist," he commented. "And where did you come from, anyway?" He'd spent weeks learning the house and its surroundings. No small gray cat had caught his attention anywhere. "Ah, you're magic. That's it, isn't it?"

With a flick of her tail the cat jumped to the floor again. His gaze, though, remained on the windowsill and the oddly shaped object leaning in its corner. Stripping off his gloves again, he walked up to the window.

For some reason, even after hearing Isabel describe the mysterious missing orb at least a half dozen times, he'd pictured it as being round. The smooth, milky-white stone, though, was oval. A bit smaller than his fist, it was nestled in a delicate gold setting of eagle or owl – or dragon, he supposed – claws reaching up from the base.

It felt, in an odd, dreamy way, like the house – old, but ageless. Frowning, he picked it up. The sun through the windows had warmed the stone's surface, and a rainbow of iridescence shone through its depths. Whatever it was rumored to be it was lovely, and for that reason alone he could see why Isabel had been so determined to locate it.

Adam held it up to eye it more closely. "Aren't you supposed to speak the name of my true love now?" he asked. "Or do you only do that for Nimue's daughters?"

The even more pressing question was how the devil it had come to be on his windowsill. He hadn't spent a particular amount of time looking in that exact spot, but he was also reasonably sure it hadn't been there this morning – or any time before that. But every servant in the household knew the legend of the orb. If one of them had found it, he or she would not have simply left it behind in his bedchamber.

It made no sense. He looked around for the cat and found her sitting beside the door. The orb was fairly solid, even with a hollowed-out bottom. A small cat wouldn't have been able to haul it about, much less jump three feet into the air with it in her mouth.

"If you're waiting for me to ask you where this came from," he muttered at Mist, pulling a pressed cravat from a drawer and wrapping it about the orb, "don't bother. I'm not asking you. You're a cat."

Mist preceded him out of his bedchamber and led the way downstairs to his makeshift office. The butler crossed his path, as did one of the downstairs maids, but he did nothing more than nod at them. The carefully wrapped item in his hand belonged to Isabel de Rossi, and she should be the first – or second, rather – to know about it.

And if she or someone else had secretly found it and then placed it on his windowsill to prove the existence of magic or some sort, he hadn't lost his mind or his sense of logic and reason. For the moment the orb's reappearance remained merely unexplained.

He closed himself inside the small room then carefully placed the orb behind a selection of books on an upper shelf. No one in their right mind would have reason to delve into crop rotations in the Lake District today.

That done, he turned to find Mist standing on his desk, looking at him. "Not a word from you, either," he ordered, ruffling the little cat behind the ears as he walked past to open the door again. "I'm shutting this, so you'd best come out unless you want to be trapped in here all day."

With a distinct huff the cat joined him in the hallway, only to lie down with her back against the door the moment he closed it. *Hmm.* He had no objection if Mist wanted to guard his door. Or simply nap there, which seemed more likely. That done, he pulled on his gloves again and went to help level the ground at the back of the house in preparation for its new orangery.

It was past noon when one of the kitchen staff appeared with glasses of lemonade and sandwiches for him and the two Stephenses. Giving her a grateful smile, Adam found a shady spot of grass beneath an elm tree and well away from the beehive and sat with a groan. The bees seemed to have settled in, but he didn't feel like getting chased into the lake again on the slight chance he was wrong.

"I spoke to Mr. Hayward," a cool, feminine voice said from the far side of the tree. "You ordered two of his box hives."

Despite the slight tremor through his chest that Isabel's voice caused, he had to note that she'd placed herself in such a way that she couldn't even see him. So now they weren't even looking at each other, apparently. "I did. I can cancel the order if you've changed your mind about Top Drawer Hon—"

"Thank you," she interrupted, her skirt rustling as she turned away.

For a single heartbeat he considered not telling her about the orb, letting her continue her fruitless search of the Hall. In the next second, though, he set aside his luncheon and stood. "If you have a moment, there's something you should see."

As he rounded the tree she stopped, her back to him. This couldn't continue; another day or two of being so clearly despised and he would simply have to tender his resignation. But for today, he would tolerate it. He bloody well wasn't apologizing for being honest, and that was for damned certain.

"I have *a* moment," she returned stiffly.

"My office, then."

He followed her inside to find Mist still blocking the closed door. Before he could shoo the cat out of the way Isabel crouched and scooped it into her arms. "There you are, you sneaky thing," she said, kissing the top of its head. "I haven't seen you since yesterday."

Adam reached around the two of them to open the door, carefully not noting the way the top of Isabel's head came just to his chin. It didn't matter, because as good-hearted and lovely as she was, she was also only a petal or two short of being a blooming lunatic. "She followed me into my bedchamber this morning when I returned from the market. Jumped up onto my windowsill. When I—"

"Cats do like the sun, Mr. Driscoll. You needn't regale me with her every movement." She set Mist down, and the cat promptly leaped up onto his desk again, her tail up as she fixed her gaze on his bookshelf. "By the way, I'll be joining Lord Alton for luncheon at the Two-Headed Dragon on Wednesday. Please arrange to have the curricle and a driver for me."

"So Geoffrey flattered you with some speech about the mysteries of Somerset, and Glastonbury Cathedral being the mythological burial spot for Arthur and Guinevere, did he?" he snapped back, then shut his mouth again. *Damnation*. He hadn't meant to let Alton beneath his skin. Because of course Geoffrey would push for a second rendezvous. She had something he wanted. The only question as far as Adam was concerned was what that thing was.

She faced him, her chin lifted and her cheeks red – more from anger than embarrassment, if he had to wager a guess. "Geoffrey," she enunciated, "grew up here. And yes, he knows a great deal about the area. And he's not nearly as closed-minded as some people. And as you are not my brother to decide with whom I should or should not spend my time, I'll thank you to keep your opinions to yourself."

That did it.

"No, I'm not your damned brother," he growled, crossing to her in two long steps. Adam took her shoulders in his hands, and as she looked up at him, startled, he leaned down and kissed her. Her lips were as soft as he'd imagined, and tasted faintly of some chocolate treat she'd no doubt sampled at the market.

Knowing he would never be this close to her again, he shifted a hand to one soft cheek, tilting her face up to deepen the embrace of their mouths. Even stubborn and absurd he wanted her, and his body yowled in protest at what his honor wouldn't allow. This was going too far, and as his mind caught up to his actions he wrenched himself backward, away from her.

Turning away, stalking for the door so he wouldn't see the shock and dismay on her face, he wiped a hand across his mouth. "Look behind the Lake District book for what I found this morning," he said flatly, not wanting her to think he'd been hiding it out of spite or something. Forcing a kiss on her was bad enough.

"You'll have my letter of resignation within the hour. I'll be gone by sunset."

With that he left the room, shutting the door firmly behind him. He'd destroyed his career, and his future at Nimway Hall, in exchange for a momentary daydream. And as little as he believed in flights of fancy or indulging fictions, he couldn't say that it hadn't been worth it.

CHAPTER 9

*I*sabel stood, her eyes and her mouth and her hands open, staring at the closed door of Adam Driscoll's little office. Abruptly she gulped in air, wondering when, exactly, she'd stopped breathing.

She was half-Italian, raised among free-spirited artists. And she was eighteen years old. Of course she'd been kissed before. But not like that. Those had been…boys, the kisses clumsy and damp. Not heat and pull and desire.

Blinking, she sat down hard in the chair behind the small, simple desk. *What the deuce had just happened?* The – He – She should be furious. He hadn't asked, but suddenly she'd been in his arms, and she'd liked being there. She'd been mad at him for calling her childish, and then… Good heavens.

Had it been jealousy? She'd just told him – well, flaunted it in front of him, really – that she'd ignored his warnings about Lord Alton and would be joining the viscount for luncheon. But…

She stood up again. Adam Driscoll needed to be dismissed immediately. She needed to dismiss him. And slap him. But he'd just resigned, hadn't he? Trying to slow down the swirl of her thoughts, she pushed against all the noise banging at her mind.

Yes, he'd said he would write his resignation letter and be gone by sunset. And something about books on the Lake District, though what that had to do with kissing her, she had no idea.

Taking another deep breath, she walked to the window. *Think,* she demanded. He'd found something, he'd said. Or Mist had. And he'd put it with the Lake District books. That was it.

Isabel returned to the bookcase. Books about grain, sheep, watermills, tree growth and health…and crop rotation in the Lake District. With her fingers still not quite steady, she reached up and pulled it down. Something bulky and white lay on the shelf behind it.

After removing another two books, she carefully reached to the back of the shelf and pulled down the white-wrapped bundle. Seeing the size of it and feeling its weight, she could guess what it might be. What she wanted it to be. Her heart couldn't pound any harder without it exploding from her chest, and for the second time in five minutes she had to take a seat.

He'd wrapped it in what looked like a cravat, and for a good minute she sat there, gazing at the bundle in her lap. Mist had moved to sit at the edge of the desk, her green gaze fixed either on the cravat or on what lay concealed inside it.

"Did *you* find this?" Isabel asked the cat. "He was telling me what you were up to." And now she wished she'd let him finish instead of choosing to bait him with her luncheon.

No, no. She hadn't been baiting him. That implied that she'd wanted him to react, that she liked when she caught him looking at her and the way he simply assumed her to be smart and competent. But she'd only wanted him to know, of course, that she was a grown woman perfectly capable and willing to make her own decisions. For heaven's sake, she'd never thought that would lead to him kissing her.

"Stop it," she muttered. This bundle in her lap was in all probability the orb – the magical thing that had brought her parents and her grandparents and her great-grandparents together. The thing that would show her who her true love was.

And instead of looking at it, she was thinking about that aggravating man.

She unwrapped the bundle carefully, begrudgingly grateful that Adam – Mr. Driscoll – had taken such care with it. And then there it was, gold talons rising up from the base to clutch the milky stone above it. "Oh, my," she breathed, setting aside the cravat. This…orb, so old no one could say for certain what it was, belonged to her now. The land was hers, yes, and the responsibility that came with it, but this – this was the center of it all. The magic, the promise, the heart.

Holding her breath, she gripped it firmly in both hands and lifted it. The moonstone glowed softly, flecks of rainbow iridescence glinting in its depths, a swirl of light that reminded her more of sunlight through deep shade than candle- or firelight.

The stupid man who didn't believe in magic should see this. He would only insist it was a trick of sun and mirrors or something, of course. *Ha.* She stood, walking to the window just to reassure herself that she wasn't imagining things. The internal light remained unchanged, no matter how she twisted or turned.

"Show me with whom I'm meant to be," she urged, studying the depths beneath the well-polished surface.

As she watched, the glow dimmed into regular sunlight, once more just an unusual, pretty bauble. She didn't know precisely how it was supposed to work, but she was fairly certain it hadn't done what it was meant to. Isabel gave it a gentle shake. "Show me Lord Alton," she insisted, moving away from the window again. "Or say his name. Geoffrey Bell-Spratt."

Nothing. Frowning, she set it upright on the desk, shook out her hands, and picked it up again. Now for all the response she got, she might as well have been holding a paperweight.

Had she broken it? Had its magic faded after so many centuries? Or had it felt Adam Driscoll's cynicism and wooden-headedness and decided the lot of them unworthy? Oh, he was so blasted aggravating! First to call her little more than a naïve child then five days later to kiss her and find the object with which she'd been obsessed for her entire life... What was she supposed to make of that?

As she paced the orb slowly warmed in her fingers, the light of its depths mesmerizing. Thank goodness Adam hadn't broken it with his lack of imagination. As far as she could tell, he was the only one on her property who didn't believe that the object in her hands held magic. Even the well-educated Lord Alton believed in the possibilities. She very much doubted Geoffrey would doubt what his own eyes saw when she showed him the orb.

The light faded again. Isabel glanced at the cat. "You saw it, didn't you?"

Mist licked one paw and yawned.

Well, Isabel had seen it. Carefully she wrapped it again. It worked; she just didn't yet understand how or why. The only thing she knew about it for certain, in fact, was where it had turned up – and not even that made sense.

She supposed some well-meaning servant might have placed it in Adam's room after discovering it, but the household all looked on the steward as an outsider. If someone else with matchmaking in mind had discovered it, it seemed far more likely that it would have gone to Lord Alton for him to reveal to her, or directly to her so that Adam wasn't involved at all.

Why had the orb revealed itself to him, then? Did he have some part yet to play? Perhaps her mother and father had last been together at Nimway in that room. But Adam had kissed her. Perhaps *that* show of affection or whatever it was had been prompted by the orb's appearance – though she hoped it wouldn't have that affect on everyone. Everyone kissing willy-nilly could be very disconcerting.

"A simple name would suffice," she grumbled, deciding the thing would be safest in her bedchamber while she deciphered what its intermittent glowing meant.

In the meantime, Adam Driscoll was packing his things to leave. His absence, especially after that kiss, would make some things much simpler – he didn't believe, and she didn't like having to explain why accepting the possibility of magic made the world so much more...livable. Special.

On the other hand, he knew Nimway Hall. He knew what needed to be seen to, and how to do it. They were to meet with an architect tomorrow, and while the creative ideas they'd written up had been hers, he'd figured out the foundation and dimensions. Even more to the point, his purpose here wasn't merely to move bees. He kept the property in good order, kept it functioning. And that, at this moment, made him a better guardian than she knew how to be.

With Mist on her heels, she hurried to her bedchamber and hid the orb in a stack of pelisses, then made her way to Adam's room. This was for Nimway, she reminded herself, ignoring the fact that she might have waited for him to appear in the foyer or the front drive. This was important. This was her first step toward being a worthy guardian.

Isabel knocked. For a silent moment she thought he'd left already; he was very efficient, after all. Then the door wrenched open and he stood there, jaw clenched and his dark-brown hair a bit disheveled, green eyes widening a little as he looked down at her. "I told you I'm leaving," he said stiffly.

"I heard you."

"I don't have much here; I assure you, I'll be well away within the hour."

"I have two things to say to you," she returned. "And I believe you owe me your attention."

One eye twitched. "I'm listening."

"Firstly, thank you for delivering the orb to me. I know it had to go against your firm belief in the pedestrian."

Both eyes narrowed now. "You want to continue to argue? For the devil's sake, Miss de Rossi, I'm leaving. Live in the fantasy you wish. I won't be here to poke at it."

"Secondly," she pushed, resisting the urge to tell him what she'd witnessed with the moonstone. He wouldn't believe it, anyway. "My plan when I arrived here, my idea to serve as a guardian to Nimway Hall, was far more...short-sighted than I'd realized. You overstepped, sir, and yes, you should be sacked for it. However, I propose a way for you to make amends, to erase this blemish."

He folded his arms over his chest. "Do you, then?"

Intimidation? Oh no, she didn't think so. Not after what she'd just witnessed with the orb. "Teach me what I need to know. Show me how to be Nimway's steward, or at least what to look for when I hire your replacement. I shall continue to pay your current salary for your time. *Then* leave, with a letter of recommendation from me."

Adam tilted his head to study her face. For what, she had no idea. "And the kiss?" he asked finally.

"We'll never speak of it again. It's already forgotten."

More gazing at her. "Two months," he said abruptly.

"We're negotiating, then? Four months." She didn't know if the idea that he was mulling over the offer annoyed or pleased her, but he was clearly doing so. "And I remind you that your actions are the reason we've come to this conversation." *There.*

"You said you'd already forgotten about my actions. Have you not?"

Maddening. But she still needed him. "We would not be having this conversation if you hadn't acted as you did. That is a fact. Otherwise, yes. I consider it forgotten."

"Then four months is acceptable."

Oh. *Oh.* She'd won. Isabel stuck out her hand. "We have a deal, Mr. Driscoll."

He unfolded his arms and took her hand in his large, rough one, shaking it. "It's still Adam. And if you're hiring me to instruct you, I do expect you to listen to what I say. You're the guardian of Nimway Hall. I'm your...tutor."

This wasn't quite the contrition or apology she'd expected from him for his poor behavior, but it was what she – and the Hall – needed. "Agreed. And I remain Isabel."

Adam released her hand. "Shall we begin in the morning? Seven o'clock at the stable?"

"I'll be there."

He could have said three o'clock in the morning and she would have agreed. In some ways, this revised agreement left her feeling easier than the previous one. She didn't have to feel guilty that she would eventually be sending him on his way, that she was secretly learning what she could from him without telling him so. And this way he would tell her everything she needed to know instead of leaving great gaps for her to attempt to decipher because she couldn't come out and ask him directly.

"Was there something else, Isabel?"

She blinked. Drat it all, she still stood there, staring at him. "No. You make the schedule according to your – my – duties, and I shall follow it."

"Then I have some unpacking to do. I'll arrange to take my dinner in here tonight, as I imagine you and Miss Jane will wish to discuss things without me being present. I'll see you in the morning, and don't forget Mr. Hodgins will be arriving tomorrow afternoon."

With that, he closed his door on her.

Isabel sagged against the wall. He remained direct but polite, both of which qualities she continued to appreciate. He hadn't leered or said anything overly familiar – though if he had, she would have withdrawn the offer and found someone else. In fact, the only things she could criticize were the kiss – well, not the kiss itself, but the fact that he'd kissed her – and the way he'd said it was inappropriate but hadn't precisely apologized for doing it.

But then she hadn't been quite as offended as she probably should have been. Surprised, yes. Mortified, no. Possibly intrigued despite his unsuitability, perhaps.

❧

ADAM STIFLED a yawn as he and Orion, Isabel and Fiore behind them, trotted down the path that led into Balesboro Wood and the loggers' hut within. Yes, he was the one who'd decided they should begin at seven o'clock, but he hadn't anticipated lying, tossing, standing, and pacing awake all night.

Isabel had bloody well surprised him yesterday. At best he'd thought she might realize his idiocy for the mad slip of propriety it had been, and that she would ask him to stay on for a few days while she found a replacement. He would have agreed to that.

Instead, she'd set aside her own pride twice over and asked for his help. She hadn't suggested that he work for free in exchange for her not telling everyone far and wide that he'd mauled her like some mannerless beast. She hadn't asked for a promise of his silence about her ignorance of her duties, despite the damage he could do with just a few words to her tenants.

All of that made Isabel de Rossi either the worst negotiator in history, or a genuinely good-hearted young lady who wanted to live up to the responsibilities she'd voluntarily assumed. And he already knew which she was, because he'd realized that about her days ago.

And none of that, including his gratitude at being offered a second chance, made him regret kissing her. Yes, it had been ham-fisted, and yes, he should have asked – and waited for – her permission. The kiss itself, though, he didn't regret. He would never regret it.

She would probably spin the moonstone orb until it pointed at Alton, until she could claim that magic decreed she should marry a handsome viscount, of all people. But he didn't believe in magic. He believed in that kiss. And he had four months now to convince her that the only real magic in the world lay in the way he'd felt – and the way he was willing to wager she'd felt – in that moment.

Because whether she would ever admit it or not, the real reason she wanted to pretend the kiss had never happened, and the reason he was still here today, was because she'd kissed him back.

~

"Nimway Hall holds the rights to supply all the timber to the bishoprics of both Bath and Wells, yes?" Isabel asked.

"Yes. For all the property and buildings owned by the church in both towns. It's the most lucrative piece of paper you own. Which, in all likelihood, is why Balesboro Wood is still one of the few places you can find old-growth timber in the southern half of England. I'd wager it's the largest standing natural wood in all of Britain. Your ancestors have been very careful and strategic with their tree-felling and replanting."

"It feels old," she said, ducking beneath a branch as they followed the narrowing path deeper into the forest. "Like the house."

"Ageless," he supplied, as an owl hooted above their heads. The fellow was awake late, and the sound reminded Adam of the odd owl choir that had greeted Isabel's arrival to the Hall last week.

"Yes. Ageless." She sent him a sideways glance. "Have you heard any of the local tales about these woods?"

"That they confuse unwanted travelers and turn them about to keep them from ever reaching Nimway Hall? Yes, I've heard them. I pointed out to Simmons a few weeks ago when he was lamenting the arrival of an outsider to the Hall that *I* managed to make it through the woods unscathed."

He'd thought that might set her back up, but she only smiled. "Perhaps you were meant to arrive here, to show me how to be her guardian."

And now she was trying to bait *him*. "I won't argue with that, because it ends with me being here."

"You like Nimway, then? Even with all the trouble it's given you? Even with all the myths and legends surrounding it?"

"Myths and legends come with age. I like that it's been here since before records were kept. I like the idea that its survival through the ages is so unlikely that the locals had to come up with a magical explanation for it." He mulled over what he'd just said.

"In that sense, I suppose I do believe in magic. And I'm very fond of Nimway."

"Careful. Your head may pop off if you say such things." She chuckled, then straightened in the sidesaddle. "Is that the loggers' hut?" she asked, pointing with black-gloved fingers at a misshapen lump perched beside a small stream.

"It is." They crossed through the trickle of water and pulled up at the front of the building. "It should be unoccupied at this time of year. Unless a special order is received, most logging should be done in the winter. The sap's down in the ground, so the timber dries more quickly, and you'll have less sap stain and fungus. After it's cut, it goes into the old barn by the escarpment to keep it out of the worst of the weather."

"If the hut is empty, why are we here?" she asked, hopping to the ground and taking an awkward step before he could move around Orion to assist her.

Adam frowned. If the idea of them kissing dismayed her, he needed to do something about it immediately. "Nothing nefarious," he said in a too-abrupt tone. "I erred yesterday, Isabel. I shall do my utmost not to unsettle you again."

She nodded. "I wouldn't be here if I thought otherwise. And neither would you."

Good. Frightening her, distressing her, went against everything he believed. With the exception of the past few weeks, he knew he was good at what he did. That was what she wanted from him – knowledge. If he wanted something else, something more, that was his burden to bear. Beneath all that, however, he was a male. If he saw any signs that she was as intrigued as he was, he would act.

"You or someone you trust should come by and check the condition of the hut and the tools inside every other month or so," he made himself continue, deliberately moving a little away from her. "You don't want to discover in December that the roof's fallen in and the saws have rusted from exposure to the weather, or that they've gone missing just when you need them."

Isabel nodded, a strand of her dark hair coming loose from its pins to caress one cheek. Wrinkling her nose, she drew it behind her ear. "I should have brought a pencil and paper."

"I'm happy to repeat anything you wish." Including that kiss. Especially that kiss. He realized he still had his gaze on her face, and cleared his throat, moving to the door. "I'll give you the calendar I began when I arrived here, for scheduling when to do the tasks like this. The trick is the unexpected things and how to fit them in. And the new items you discover as you go along."

"Like rooms full of bees?"

He laughed, supremely relieved that she remained willing to jest with him, as he put a shoulder to the hut's door and shoved it open. "Yes. Exactly like that."

The hut was low and long, closed in enough that he wouldn't have wanted to spend an extended length of time living there. Racks and shelves at the rear held saws, axes, ropes, spikes, and the like. The front contained the small fireplace for cooking and warmth, while four empty bedframes lined either wall down the length of the single room. A trio of rickety chairs stood tilted on the stone hearth to keep their feet out of the dirt and damp, and he pulled two of them upright, sitting them across the hut from each other before he sat on one and gestured her to the other.

With a glance about the hut that he had to interpret as uneasiness, she seated herself. Hands folded primly in her lap, feet flat on the floor and ankles touching, she looked young. And vulnerable.

"You have nothing to fear from me," he reiterated, deciding that getting to the point outweighed any of the polite dictates of small talk.

"So you said. Of course I don't." Her short laugh sounded nervous, especially coupled with her sudden interest in viewing the unremarkable fireplace.

"You and I have one disagreement," he went on. "In everything else, we do want the same thing. We want Nimway Hall to prosper. We want you to be her guardian, whether it's as a landlord – lady – or as a mythical chosen one."

"That's well and good," she returned, finally meeting his gaze. "It doesn't dismiss your…lack of physical restraint. I know I said I've put it behind me, and I have, but I'm not a fool. A certain wariness is to be expected, don't you think?"

"I do. And I've contemplated that kiss several times. Rather fondly. I might wish to repeat it, but I wouldn't do so unless you wanted the same thing."

"You—"

"In this place, under these circumstances, Isabel, you are the queen of the realm. I am in your employ. Your tenants would happily chase me out of Somerset, encouraging me with pitch-forks and torches. Yes, I'm attracted to you. I want you. But I have no intention of grabbing you and having you against your will. Therefore, you have no reason to fear me."

She swallowed. "This is rather unsettling."

He wanted to point out that he would also like to break her pretty viscount in half, but suggestions of violence wouldn't do much to keep him about for the four months to which they'd agreed. And it wouldn't convince her to trust him – though neither would regaling her with his theory that she was unsettled because she couldn't stop contemplating their kiss, either.

"Everything else aside, Isabel, the question I need you to answer is whether you can trust me or not. Not just my opinion, but *me*. Because whatever you've hired me to do, I won't have you cringing whenever I look in your direction. Have Miss Jane accompany us, or one of the grooms. Or give me a few days, and I'll find someone else to take over my duties."

Sitting forward, resting his elbows on his knees, he clasped his hands together. "I never told you my credentials," he went on. "My uncle lost a leg shortly after my eighteenth birthday. Uncle William has a plenitude of daughters, but no sons. I was the youngest of four boys, with the other three married already. My oldest brother, Thomas, will have my father's barony, and he's been working with my next brother, Donald, to expand the Driscoll holdings. Patrick, the closest in age to me, is the pastor for our home village. I'd been planning on joining the army, but that changed when we received word about Uncle William."

She seemed to be paying attention, at least, and the cautious expression had left her face, replaced by one of curiosity. That was something, anyway. "I served as his steward for the next seven years, until my oldest cousin married. Her new husband worked with me for six months, then my uncle and I agreed that Stanley should take over the stewardship. The property's likely to go to him and Margaret anyway, so it made sense. Less than a fortnight later, I accepted the position here."

"How many daughters does your uncle have?" she asked.

That hadn't been the question he'd expected, but Isabel de Rossi had never been short of surprises. "Seven. All between eighteen and twelve. Two sets of them are twins."

"And you're one of four boys. I can't even imagine having that many siblings."

"You're an only child, yes?"

"Yes. We always had friends and extended family about, but it's not the same as having siblings, is it?"

"No, it's not."

She glanced down at her hands. "I should mistrust you. Even dislike you. But I...I don't, which has me questioning my own judgment. You don't believe in magic, but you gave me the orb when you found it. I might say it found *you*, but that seems rather unlikely even to me."

Adam sent her a rueful smile. "Thank you for that."

"You're welcome. And just now you announced that you... desire me. I..." She cleared her throat. "I find you to be handsome, and I like your direct manner of speaking, but that one difference you say lies between us is an entire philosophy. A view of the world and what lies within it. That's a large difference."

Nor was he a titled lord, but he didn't say that aloud. She didn't need to be reminded about Alton, his title, and his professed belief in faeries and flying pigs. "I can't dispute that," he said instead. "Speaking of the orb, though, have you received any insight now that it's in your possession?" There. No insults to magic or to her beliefs, and no suggestion that he'd altered his own opinion.

"That was quite diplomatic," she noted, a smile touching her mouth.

Bloody wonderful. Now he was noticing her mouth again – not that he'd ever stopped noticing it. "I favor peace between us, whatever else lies unresolved."

"I favor peace as well. And no, I haven't learned anything conclusive."

Both his eyebrows lifted before he could rein in his surprise. "Truly?" He would have been willing to wager good money that she had magically been told or shown – or whatever the orb did – that Alton was the man she was destined to marry. That seemed to be what *she* wanted, at the least.

"Well, it's very old, and it's been…away, or out of sight, for twenty years. I imagine deciphering how it works will take me a little time."

"It's broken, then?" Again he refrained from commenting that a piece of pretty moonstone that did nothing was, in fact, what a piece of moonstone was supposed to do.

"No. It's not broken. Both my grandmother and my mother warned me that it does as it will, when it will." She sighed. "Grandmama Olivia said the entire house was the same way, but I think she resisted it more than she needed to. I, for one, could use some blasted guidance!"

As she spoke that last bit she lifted her gaze toward the ceiling. Adam, though, didn't think it was God or the heavenly angels from whom she wanted to hear. If her Merlin or Nimue had ever actually lived, which he doubted, they were long past hearing from her.

He cleared his throat. "You've hired me to give you some guidance where Nimway Hall is concerned, and I'm happy to do so.

And if I may say so, I'm proud to work for an owner who takes such an interest in her property. The position of steward exists in many cases because of landowners who'd rather spend their time and attention elsewhere."

"Or because they have more than one property and can't manage them all adequately," she added.

Well, he knew to whom that referred. Adam inclined his head. "Indeed." And whether he disagreed with her assessment of Alton or not, which he did, that wasn't the point. As they'd both noted, he was her employee. He had no say over what she thought or did. It certainly wasn't his responsibility or right to approve with whom she spent her time or to whom she gave her heart. Even if he'd already given most of his heart to her.

CHAPTER 10

"*L*et me see it, then," Jane said, her flailing hands jerking in an odd motion somewhere between crossing herself and making the sign of protection against the evil eye.

Isabel wanted to see the orb again as well, wanted to have a witness when it indicated whether she was right to allow Alton to pursue her, or if some as yet un-met stranger lay in her future. The third alternative was just silly, whether he confessed to being attracted to her or not, because he didn't even believe.

That in itself would eliminate him from beau contention. It didn't even take into account the way he seemed as rough around the edges as she was. It had genuinely surprised her that he was a baron's son, because he spoke and acted more like a farmer. And someone of her limited social skills and even more limited connections shouldn't set herself after a farmer. Or permit one to pursue her.

Trying to keep her hands from shaking, she opened the wardrobe and dug her hand into the folded stack of pelisses – and felt nothing but material. "What the devil?" she muttered, reaching in farther to pull out the entire pile and set it on her bed.

"Are you certain you hid it in the pelisses?" Jane asked,

hovering nearby but obviously reluctant to put herself in a situation where she might have to touch the orb. "Your shifts would be less likely to be disturbed, don't you think?"

Ignoring that, Isabel began pulling garments off the stack and shaking them out – despite the obvious weight and size of the object she sought. Halfway down the pile the balled-up cravat shook free and plopped to the floor. Cursing, she bent down and looked under the bed for good measure before she picked it up and shook it out in turn. She found no other sign of the potato-sized stone set in gold claws.

"It was wrapped up in this," she said, wadding the cravat in her fist. The fast beat of her heart pummeled the inside of her ribs, intensifying the ache in the pit of her stomach. "Who would take it? Why?"

"Who even knew you had it? You only told me about it five minutes ago."

"I didn't tell anyone!" she exclaimed, pushing back against angry, frustrated tears. For most of her eighteen years she'd longed to set eyes on the orb, and after one quick view it was snatched from her again. She nearly hadn't told Jane, but after a sleepless night she decided someone else needed to know where she'd hidden it.

"So just Mr. Driscoll knew, then?"

"He was with me all day, and he didn't know it was in my wardrobe. Mist knew; you might as well accuse her of carrying it off." She looked around her bedchamber. "Where is Mist?"

"Vanished with the orb?" Jane suggested unhelpfully.

Isabel didn't want to believe that, but in light of her arguments with Adam, she supposed she had to consider it. After all, he claimed it had to be one or the other – magic existed, or it didn't. He said it didn't, at all, in any form. The other side, then, meant that it did, in everything. Which meant the orb and the cat, which had each just seemed to appear, could just as easily disappear again. "But why?" she asked aloud.

"Perhaps you don't need it, because you've found Lord Alton on your own."

"Then why would it appear at all?" Isabel countered, diving back into the depths of the wardrobe just on the chance it might have rolled out from the pelisses.

"Because you expected it to?"

"That makes no sense. Dash it all."

Simmons took that moment to rap on her half-open door. "Miss Isabel, Mr. Hodgins has arrived. I showed him into your office as you requested." The butler paused. "I took the liberty of opening a window in the room. The fellow has the distinct odor of mildew about him."

Oh, dear. "Thank you, then. And please inform Adam of the architect's arrival."

"I passed Mr. Driscoll on the stairs. I believe he went to fetch your notes."

And by the time she made it downstairs he would likely have already given Mr. Hodgins all the information he required. She smiled at Simmons, but cursed to herself beneath it. Adam had said the orangery was her project, that he was merely her tutor. Men were impossible. "I'll be down in just a moment," she managed, when the butler shifted in the doorway.

When she turned away from the door, Jane stood there smiling at her. "Just look at you, Miss Isabel. Here for a week, and already doing renovations."

"Grandmama Olivia did renovations. I'm only adding a room to the back because I miss the scent of oranges and the taste of honey." Truth be told, she also missed her mother's warm, supportive presence. Perhaps that was why the blasted orb's re-disappearance aggravated her so. She'd wanted guidance. And now all she had was herself and too-indulgent Jane.

The blue- and-yellow pelisse she donned over her darker-blue muslin looked both practical and fashionable, she decided. If at least her wardrobe had her appearing competent, it would be an improvement over how she felt. Adding an addition to a building that had stood as long as this one abruptly felt the height of hubris. Cleaning up the paint and wallpaper, updating the dining room fireplace, that was one thing. Altering the building was another entirely. Why did she keep insisting on diving straight into water well over her head?

Oh, now she was hoping Adam *had* gone in to meet Mr. Hodgins already, and that he'd detailed every bit of what she wanted. Then she could blame any failure on him. But that made her weak and cowardly, and that would never do, either.

"You're fidgeting," Jane observed.

"I am not. I don't want to appear over eager. This is a business transaction." Smoothing the front of her muslin gown once more, she squared her shoulders and marched for the door. "Please look around for the orb again, Jane. I know you think it may turn you into a frog or something, but you need not touch it; just try to locate it."

"I will. If I find it, I'll bundle it up in a blanket and carry it with me. I won't even set it down until you and I are face-to-face."

Well, that was very brave of her, however unlikely Isabel considered the frog transmogrification possibility. "Thank you. I'll be down in my office."

At the last moment she remembered to collect the pencil and the journal she'd begun after returning from the logging hut. Thus far Adam had proved to be a willing font of valuable information, and she didn't want to miss any tidbits she might hear during the meeting.

She headed downstairs and attempted to come up with something pithy to say as she joined the meeting, only to catch sight of Adam standing in front of her office door. It wasn't the armload of rolled and folded papers he carried that caught her attention, or the sudden realization that he'd waited for her to arrive before entering the room. Rather, it was the proper coat and waistcoat he'd donned, together with a simply tied cravat. In fact, he looked a proper gentleman – which she now knew him to be, considering that his father was a baron. He was also a handsome man with grass-green eyes and a mop of hair even darker than hers, a strong chin and straight nose, and artfully arched eyebrows.

If not for his calloused hands and hard, chiseled muscles earned through nearly a decade of daily laboring, he wouldn't have been at all out of place in Almack's, she imagined, though she'd never set foot there herself. And while not a fan of irony, it didn't escape her notice that the very things she found most attractive about him were the ones that made them a poor match.

"Ready?" he asked, shaking her out of her wandering reverie. "Nod at me if you wish me to add something."

So she was to lead the conversation? Her head was swirling with all the changing expectations she harbored for herself. Well, this was her property. And it wasn't just about missing the smell of oranges, whatever she'd said to Jane. They had bees, wanted orange blossom honey, and needed a way to make it all work.

"Yes, I'm ready."

For the next three hours they talked with the mildew-odored Mr. Hodgins, who didn't know anything about the legend of Nimway Hall, but did appreciate it as a well-made piece of architecture. By the end she was exhausted, but they had a plan, and she'd hired an architect.

She gave over a downstairs sitting room close by the rear of the house for Mr. Hodgins to work, and a bedchamber in the west wing for him to set up temporary residence. The bedchamber was across the entire length of the house from hers, and while aloud she could say she wanted to give the man some privacy, it had more to do with his odor.

"Why does he smell like that?" she asked, as she and Adam saw Mr. Hodgins off in his curricle with plans to return in the next two days bearing everything he would need to begin his designs and remain in residence for at least the next two months.

Adam chuckled, gesturing for her to precede him into the house. "Perhaps it's his diet. Too much cabbage."

"Or he lives under a bridge with trolls," she added. "I hope it's his diet, because we can alter that here. Otherwise I'm ordering fresh flowers daily in every room within his vicinity."

"Poor fellow. He's a lifelong bachelor, from what I understand. He likely doesn't even notice the smell."

"Lucky him." Isabel stopped at the foot of the stairs. "Will you join us for dinner tonight?"

"I will. Thank you."

Halfway up the stairs she paused again, then turned to face him. With him three steps below her, for once she could look down at him. "I'm not going to keep inviting you every night. From now on, unless you have another engagement, I'll expect you to dine with Jane and me."

He sketched a shallow bow. "Then I shall do so."

Isabel turned around again and ascended the rest of the stairs. She hadn't extended the invitation because she liked him or anything. It was simply the proper thing to do. That thought sparked another one, and she turned around yet again as they started down the hallway to their respective bedchambers, now having to lift her chin to meet his gaze since they were on level ground. "You're a part of the household, after all."

"For the next four months, anyway," he returned. "I'll see you shortly."

His bedchamber lay several doors before Jane's, and he turned out of the hallway and went inside as Isabel continued toward the end of the hallway and her own large room. Lord Alton would have walked her all the way to her door, but then Geoffrey was skilled and practiced in all the gentlemanly arts. Adam just assumed she could manage walking another thirty feet on her own while he went off to see to more important things – like changing for dinner, she assumed.

Behind her, a door opened. "Isabel?"

She stopped. "Yes, Adam?"

Mr. Driscoll stood in his doorway, his expression...annoyed? Perplexed? She couldn't decipher it. "Would you join me for a moment?" he asked.

"I – No. That's not at all proper."

That made him scowl. "I'm not going to ravish you. I need you to see something."

Her heart began to beat in an odd, unsettling tempo. "And what, exactly, might that be?"

"Oh, for God's sake. I'll stay right here in the doorway if you want. Go look." He jabbed a finger at the interior of his bedchamber.

Now she had to accept that this wasn't a subversive attempt at romance. As for why that was the first place her thoughts went, she would decipher later. Clasping her hands behind her back, Isabel marched to his door. "Very well. Show me whatever it is you want me to see."

"Thank you." Even that short sentence sounded exasperated. He strode into the room ahead of her and jabbed a finger at his dressing table. "Did you put it there?"

She looked. *The orb.* It sat squarely in the middle of the small table, its image reflecting back to her in the mirror behind it. Mist the cat lay curled on the seat of the chair pushed up to the table, a lighter shadow amid darker ones. "No. I didn't."

"I gave it to you yesterday."

"Yes, I recall," she returned, her mind swirling with questions and possibilities. "And I went to show it to Jane before we met with Mr. Hodgins, and it was gone. Your cravat was still in my wardrobe, but it was empty. Did you take it?"

"No. As a rule I do not dig through my employer's wardrobe. Someone did, though. And that troubles me."

"If someone went to the bother of finding it, I doubt they would place it on your dressing table."

"And yet there it is. Your argument is faulty."

"And you are annoying." With a sniff she stomped over and picked it up. As her hands closed over it, the orb glowed. *Ha!* "Look!" Swiftly she whirled around, but as she held it out, the inner light faded once more.

His gaze lifted from the orb to her face. "Look at what?"

"It… Oh, never mind. You wouldn't believe it even if you saw it. That's likely why it doesn't bother with you." Stubborn, pedestrian man. "Come along, Mist. I have to dress for dinner. And find a better place to secure my treasure."

Clearly in high dudgeon she swept out of the room, the small gray cat at her heels. Adam stayed where he was, gazing at his reflection in the mirror. Gazing just where he'd been looking when she'd picked up the orb, his mind refusing to move beyond that moment. *The damned thing had glowed.*

The sun hadn't caused it; this was the east wing of Nimway Hall, and late afternoon. Reflection from a lamp? Adam supposed that was possible, but even as he considered the logical options he had to conclude that none of them made much sense. Neither, though did a glowing rock.

Perhaps she'd rubbed something phosphorescent on her hands and the moonstone. That could be it. Except that they'd spent the last three hours together and he hadn't noted anything during that time. The damned orb hadn't been there when he'd changed out of his riding attire, and he'd closed the door when he left.

The cat had found a way in, however, so at some point the door must have been opened. If he wanted answers and an explanation, then, he needed to discover who'd been entering his bedchamber – twice now, at least.

Swiftly he changed his coat for a darker one, deciding the rest of him looked well enough for dinner in the countryside. As he left the room to head downstairs he did something he hadn't bothered with since he'd arrived better than five weeks ago; he locked his door.

The likeliest culprit, the one who knew about the orb and its importance to Isabel and who had unlimited access to her and to the rest of the house, was Jane Davies. The woman seemed horribly honest and adoring of her charge, however, and he couldn't conceive of a reason she would wish to take the orb from Isabel and put it in his private quarters. Was this a very poorly planned attempt to see him let go for theft? *Hmm.* That, he could imagine. And if seeing him gone was the play, it could be anyone in the household.

None of that, though, explained the moonstone's glowing when Isabel put her hands on it. Perhaps he'd just seen it wrong after all. An illusion wasn't magic. It was simply a reality that hadn't yet been explained.

Straightening his coat, deciding "an illusion, as yet unexplained" would suffice for the night, Adam made for the upstairs drawing room that adjoined the formal dining room. The house boasted a small dining room that would have been more appropriate for three diners, but he knew Isabel liked seeing the fireplace in the larger room. And modeled after her mother or not, it was exquisite.

He poured himself a whiskey and sat on the overstuffed couch, then immediately stood again as Isabel entered the drawing room. She wore silk tonight, a deep, soft green with deeper green glass beads sewn throughout the bodice and skirt, like random, twinkling stars. Likewise a green ribbon wove through her long hair, which was drawn up into an artful tangle at the top of her head. Abruptly he felt both underdressed and overdressed – as in he would prefer to be wearing nothing, with her in his arms.

"Jane will be down in a moment," she announced, strolling to the window to view the deepening twilight.

"You look very nice tonight," he said, clenching his half-full glass hard as he walked over to join her. *Don't touch her!* he shouted at himself. Just this morning he'd promised to be a damned gentleman.

"Thank you."

They stood there, looking outside, while he searched for something clever to say to her. "The orb is secure?" he finally asked. It wasn't particularly clever, but it was conversation, at the least.

"I certainly hope so. I can think of nowhere more secret to put it, except perhaps the beehive."

Adam laughed. On their first meeting he would never have

guessed that she was funny and clever, but she was. Genuinely so. "You would know who took it from there by the bee stings. Perhaps you should consider it."

"If it disappears again, I shall. Some of my ancestors tried displaying it in a place of pride. Even with the entire household keeping an eye on it, the orb still managed to vanish."

"You believe it has a mind of its own, then?"

She slanted her eyes at him. "I'm not going to have this argument with you again."

The question had been more a matter of genuine curiosity than a comment about the way she viewed the object, but he inclined his head. "Very well. May I ask you something else, then?"

Isabel faced him. "What is it?"

He should probably keep his damned mouth shut, but she looked so lovely, and he felt so...drawn to her that he'd sooner be able to resist breathing. If he said nothing, he would have to rightfully call himself a coward. "Have you decided on Alton?"

Her cheeks darkened. "Decided on him for what?"

Adam smiled a little. "No offense meant, but you don't play coy well, Isabel."

"Hmm. I don't see what business it is of yours, then, but no, I haven't decided anything. Why?"

To hell with it. If he didn't act now, he might as well cut bait and go join the army after all. "Because I would like to invite you to join me for luncheon on Thursday."

CHAPTER 11

*S*tormy gray eyes met his, and it took every ounce of his willpower not to close the distance between them and kiss her. He'd never been in this position before, of having to step so carefully. Yes, he wanted her to see him as trustworthy, but at the same time he wasn't a damned puppy dog. She had money and property, whereas he did not. But she also claimed to believe in magic, so he had a thing or two to overlook, himself. And he was certainly willing to do just that.

"You want to…call on me?"

"Yes, I wish to call on you."

Her gaze lowered to the buttons of his waistcoat. "Because you don't approve of Alton?"

No, he damned well did not approve of Alton. "There are at least three additional male property owners – or their sons, rather – in the area without wives," he returned, not terribly thrilled to be pointing that out. "Alton's merely the first to come calling. He may have warned away the others, for all I know. I don't answer to him, though."

"No, you answer to me."

Adam nodded. "That, I do. And I happen to like you and

admire you, and I would like to chat with you about something other than logs or bees."

"Friends could chat about more than logs and bees any time they wished."

"Friends could. And I think we are becoming friends. Do friends contemplate kisses and sex and marriage and children?"

Her already-pink cheeks darkened further. "Do you contemplate those things?"

"Yes. Don't you?"

Perhaps he didn't merit her. Without taking into account personality or morality or...humanity, the viscount did have more to offer. Money, for example. And a title. But even if Adam didn't feel drawn to her, he couldn't in good conscience leave her without at least a fair warning – even if he couldn't go into specifics.

"I like you, Isabel. A great deal. At the least, you could use me as a base of comparison against Alton, or vice versa."

"But you nearly resigned just two days ago because you kissed me."

"I nearly resigned because I didn't ask your permission first. I'm asking now. You've granted Alton a luncheon; I'm not asking for any more than an equal opportunity."

"I'm beginning to feel like a chess piece."

He tilted his head. "I'm not playing games."

Isabel shifted her stance, likely trying to find her figurative footing. "The opportunity isn't precisely equal, though; I talk to you all the time. We have spent far more time together than Alton and I have."

He moved a breath closer. It was ironic that her spending more time with Alton would likely work in Adam's favor, but he didn't like the idea of it, anyway. Alton could be notoriously charming, and given the wealth of Nimway Hall, the viscount would have every reason to say all the things Isabel no doubt longed to hear. Therefore, if this *was* a game, he needed to play to win. "Is that a yes, or a no, to luncheon on Thursday?" he murmured.

"I..."

"Unless your orb has already selected Alton for you," he pushed, then realized he shouldn't have taken the magic-versus-fact tack. "I mean to say," he went on, silently cursing himself for being as stubborn about logic as she was about fantasy, "you either want to have luncheon with me, or you don't." And if she didn't, the four months he'd promised to remain at Nimway Hall would become a damned, torturous eternity.

Her sweet lips pursed, then curved into a slow smile he instantly memorized. "Then I suppose we shall have luncheon on Thursday," she breathed.

Behind them the lamps in the room flickered, sending soft candlelight playing along her face. Kisses and warm, long nights, children, laughter – it all felt so close he could nearly reach out and touch it, take hold of it, and claim it for himself. Claim her for himself.

Slowly he reached out and took her hand in his free one, setting aside his whisky with the other. He'd promised her that she needn't worry over him while they were out conducting the Hall's business. Perhaps he wasn't being completely fair now, but they weren't out anywhere alone, and this bloody well wasn't business.

When he drew her closer she didn't resist, and in fact lowered her gaze to his mouth. Adam felt like a coachman trying to rein in a quartet of very spirited horses, but he hauled back against lust, against jealousy over Alton, against the desire to tell her what her moonstone orb couldn't, because it was nothing but a damned polished rock – that the two of them belonged together.

Instead he touched his lips to hers, feeling her momentary uncertainty then the pure headiness of her kissing him back. He put both hands around her waist, moving in closer while her arms slid over his shoulders. This, this moment, felt like the unnamed thing he'd been missing from his life. An open circle, completed.

Behind them the door bumped open. "Shoo, you wicked thing!" Jane Davies stated, even as Isabel lurched backward out of his arms. "I am not apologizing for being late. That blasted cat dragged one of my shoes under my bed, then wouldn't let me down a single stair without trying to twist under my feet. I think she might be trying to murder me."

Adam sent the gray cat a grateful look as she jumped onto the back of the couch. Green eyes gazed back at him, unblinking. Evidently he owed Mist a bowl of fish stew for delaying the lady's companion. "You weren't injured, I hope," he said aloud, stepping forward as Isabel ducked behind him.

He could understand her wanting to keep the kiss a secret; she still had Alton on her fishing line, after all. He didn't like it, but he understood it. The viscount was a viscount, after all, with several estates of his own, a darling of the *ton*, and her way to become part of the social elite – if that was her goal. All Adam had to offer was his knowledge. Still, she'd used him as a shield while she composed herself, so hopefully she considered that they were partners of a sort.

"No, I'm not injured, but you need to put a bell on that little demon, Isabel."

"I've been meaning to," Isabel returned, smoothing her pretty gown as she stepped back into view. "I'll see to it tomorrow."

The glass of whisky bumped against his hand, and he closed his fingers around it. "I recall some small bells in the attic. They were attached to a rather spectacular lady's hat, I believe. One of them might suit. I'll fetch one in the morning."

"Thank you," Isabel said, more feelingly than seemed strictly necessary.

If she was thanking him for the kiss, she was quite welcome. "Well, we can't have Mist sneaking up on people," he said aloud, as Simmons opened the far door to announce dinner.

Mrs. Dall's cooking had improved since Isabel's arrival, and he didn't think it was solely because there was once again a lady of the house to decide on the menu. Everything about Nimway had improved since Isabel's arrival, but he wasn't about to put that to magic, either. The lamps shone brighter and the windows let in more light, but no doubt that was because the maids now had a reason to clean them more carefully. Likewise the fireplaces smoked less, and the chandeliers gleamed and sparkled.

His growing frustration with problems that wouldn't be repaired had vanished as well, now that the bees were gone from the spare room, the millstone mended, the roof leaking over the east wing patched, and the front of the garden cleared – and without incident – for the new orangery.

"I hope you don't mean to drive into Balesborough alone," Jane said, over a generous helping of roasted venison and onion sauce. "I know this isn't London, but it's still not seemly."

"I won't be driving myself," Isabel replied. "And Lord Alton selected a popular dining establishment. Nothing unseemly will occur. There's no need for you to stand at attention over my shoulder."

"You should still have someone else with you."

Isabel set down her fork. "Jane, this is *my* land. Mine. I am the hand that will guide it. I don't want to give the impression that I'm so frail and delicate I need to be escorted everywhere."

Jane clucked her tongue and looked over at Adam. "What do you think, Mr. Driscoll?"

He'd already spent twenty minutes trying to be invisible, because he'd recognized this trap from a mile away. "I think that Isabel traveled from Italy to Somerset with only you as her companion, and that you adore her and worry over her. And I think Isabel knows her own mind and capabilities."

With a laugh that sounded a bit sharp, Isabel picked up her glass of Madeira and toasted him. She'd already emptied the thing twice, though he wasn't certain whether that was because of the conversation or his earlier kiss. "You are a true diplomat, Adam."

That didn't much feel like a compliment, considering he was an inch away from deciding to follow her into Balesborough so he could lurk in the rafters of the Two-Headed Dragon while she dined. "Actually, I'm merely aware that you have more allies in the village than does Alton, should anything untoward happen."

"Thank goodness for that," Miss Davies said. "I told you everyone here would love you, Isabel."

Isabel, though, sent him an assessing look. "And what will you be doing tomorrow, Adam?"

"I'll be looking in on several farms to see how the rye and wheat crops are coming along," he decided, since it wouldn't put him at any one place at any particular time.

"Please report to me what you see."

He nodded. "I shall." Unless he happened to wander in the direction of Balesborough and saw a chance to disrupt a luncheon, that was.

THE DRIVE to Balesborough took a bit longer than usual despite the fine weather and the fresh pair of horses; the sheep that insisted on milling about on the road seemed at least as pleased by the day as she was. Isabel didn't begrudge the time away from learning her duties. Rather, it struck her that she could ride for an hour, past Balesborough and past East Pennard and past West Pennard, before she came to the end of her property. Remarkable. And intimidating.

Scattered farms, patches of wood, streams, meadows, hills, and flatlands, wild and cultivated – she felt all over again the immensity of the task she'd taken on, and gratitude to her grandmother for hiring Adam Driscoll to help her learn how to manage all of it.

Surreptitiously she ran a finger across her lips, feigning a cough when Billy the groom glanced over at her. All the previous night she'd been plagued by fitful dreams of floating orbs shining with the faces of every man she'd ever met, including the old, toothless donkey herder back in Florence. Everyone had been yelling at her to choose them, until they all turned into bees and flew into her wardrobe. She'd fled outside, only to have the moon

turn into a giant orb and chase her over the edge of the escarpment. She'd awakened falling out of bed.

Of course she knew what the blasted dream meant, even if
Antonio the donkey man had never been an actual contender for
her hand. Adam, though, had spoken the word marriage, and he'd
kissed her in a way that had made her drink too much Madeira
with dinner – which had probably caused the nightmares.

She'd been away from her home and her family for less than
two months, and in that time she'd sailed through the Mediter-
ranean and the English Channel to Dover, she'd taken possession
of the papers that granted her ownership and, less officially,
guardianship, of a large estate, and she'd landed directly between
two men who both claimed to want her. And each had warned her
about the other, even if Geoffrey's vitriol over Adam had
consisted more of the "wades about in mud" and "wouldn't know
a quadrille from a gallop" sort of commentary.

Those thoughts blew away on the wind as they emerged from
a pretty stand of elm and beech trees to see the small village in the
shallow valley before them. She'd loved the sight from the first
moment Adam had led her here, and for an odd moment she
wished it were Adam driving the curricle today so she could chat
with him about why everyone seemed to have decided to visit the
village today. The delightful scent of fresh bread coming from the
direction of the bakery would have convinced her to stop in, but
goodness it was crowded.

Isabel took a breath. Today was for luncheon with Lord Alton.
For heaven's sake, with Adam's annoying lack of imagination he
could well be planning to bring her back to this very same location for his luncheon with her tomorrow. Her heart fluttered a
little. Luncheon tomorrow wouldn't be about tenants and their
trades or why the main road through the village looked as busy as
a London street. Though what in the world she and Adam would
chat about if it wasn't Nimway Hall, she had no idea.

He might speak of marriage, but nothing had occurred to
make him more suitable. For heaven's sake, when he'd kissed her

yesterday, she'd kissed him back. Her steward. Proper females did not entertain romances with their employees. By that misstep alone she'd proven how much she needed a husband who knew the nuances of Society, who could keep her ignorance secret both from their peers and her own tenants.

"There it is, Miss Isabel," Billy the driver said, lifting a hand from the leads to point at a two-story, many-windowed building perched between a bakery and a clothing shop. A small sign over one window featured a winged, rearing green dragon boasting two heads, both of them breathing orange fire.

A man in a very stylish blue beaver hat and dark-brown caped greatcoat leaned against the wall beside the door, and he stood upright as Billy drew the team to a halt. Sweeping off the hat to expose trim golden hair, he gave an elegant bow before straightening to offer her a hand.

"You are a vision, Isabel," Geoffrey said, smiling deeply. "Fit for the finest tea house in London."

"I'll take my luncheon at the bakery, Miss Isabel," Billy said from behind her. "The curricle will be just there up the street, in view."

She wondered briefly if Adam had made those arrangements, and had told the groom to remain nearby. "Thank you, Billy." Giving her hand to the viscount, she stepped down onto the brace before the near wheel and then down to the ground. At least Geoffrey hadn't grabbed her around the waist and lifted her down as if she were a bale of hay. "And thank you, Geoffrey."

"It is my absolute pleasure." He offered his arm, and she wrapped her fingers around his sleeve as they walked through a small flock of chickens and up to the old inn. A man in crisp red livery that wouldn't have been out of place in the royal court of a hundred or so years ago opened the door as they reached it, then with much bowing led them to a small table at the front of the well-lit room.

Geoffrey held her chair for her, and she sat directly beside one of the large windows that looked onto the street. From there she would be able to view anything that passed, and everyone outside would see her and in whose company she dined. If the viscount had arranged this, and she assumed he had, it was quite a public statement about the two of them.

Of course if news spread as quickly as it generally seemed to do here on her property, by the end of the meal everyone would know that she'd come to visit and with whom she'd sat, anyway. Perhaps there was no strategy to the luncheon at all, then, and all titled gentlemen who came to dine got to sit beneath the most public window of the Two-Headed Dragon.

From the looks and whispered commentary of the rest of the diners in the crowded room, she'd been correct about the village's reaction to her arrival. Anonymity was out of the question. She was therefore glad she'd decided to wear her prettiest muslin gown, a yellow- and green- and blue-flowered print with ruffled sleeves suited for both driving and for dining at a clearly well-to-do establishment.

Geoffrey seated himself opposite her after he handed off his hat, gloves, and coat to the red-liveried man. "A bottle of your finest and fruitiest red wine," he said.

The waiter bowed. "At once, my lord."

Once the man vanished, Geoffrey sat forward. "What do you think? Fairly impressive for the middle of Somerset."

"It's lovely. All the windows must cost them a small fortune."

"And it's horrifically cold in the winter. But it is *the* place in Balesborough to be seen." Reaching across the table, he touched her fingers. "Speaking of which, I've very nearly decided to hold a soiree at Blackbridge next month. Agree to come as my guest of honor, and I'll invite half the good *ton* to meet you. Most of them will have emptied out of London by then, anyway." He smiled again. "The exotic daughter of a famed Italian sculptor. You'll be the belle of the ball."

She'd dreamed of being the center of attention at a proper London ball since she'd turned eight and spent six months wearing a tiara made of glass stones and wire. But being viewed as an outsider, exotic or not, gave her the shakes. "That sounds lovely, but please don't go to all that bother on my account."

"Nonsense. In my company, you'll do splendidly. And who knows, we may even have something to announce there."

Engagement. He expected to use the ball to announce their engagement. Evidently he had everything planned out. Heavens, if she'd agreed to go to luncheon with him a week ago, they might have been betrothed already. Isabel blinked, forcing her thoughts back into order and unsure whether her elevated heartbeat was caused by anticipation or nerves.

Before she could figure it out the waiter reappeared with the wine. Geoffrey smelled the cork then tasted a mouthful, after which he permitted the man to pour them each a glass. Isabel watched it all, but if asked to recount it later she doubted she would be able to do so. The viscount seemed calm enough, but then he'd clearly put a great deal of thought into the merging path of their lives.

"'Something to announce'?" she repeated belatedly, as the waiter departed again. "That's rather bold of you, Geoffrey, considering we've only set eyes on each other thrice now."

Geoffrey sighed. "Have I erred again? When I see something and I know the likely outcome, pretending otherwise becomes rather counterproductive and needlessly tedious, don't you think?"

"What is it you know, then? Perhaps I'm simply obtuse."

The viscount chuckled. "Given your appearance and the timber rights and land you hold, my dear, you could have worse conversation than a rock and still be sought-after." He took a sip of wine. "Thankfully you're charming, and while I could spend days and weeks flattering you and bringing you poems and posies, you also already know your value. And you know we make a good match."

Isabel took a swallow of the too-sweet wine and nearly choked on it. Everything he said made sense, but it didn't...feel...particularly special. It didn't feel like the way a marriage for a guardian of

Nimway Hall should happen. "I don't require flattery, of course," she returned, smiling back at him so he wouldn't realize that a few decisive words from him had left her completely flummoxed. "I do require at least a kernel of mutual affection, however." She'd nearly said "romance", but in light of his confidence that sounded somewhat naïve.

"Oh, affection galore," he stated. "I adore you already, of course." He glanced out the window as if something had caught his attention, then looked back at her. "Thank you for reminding me that even if something is a foregone conclusion, it shouldn't be taken for granted. It's not every day, after all, that a gentleman meets a descendant of Merlin himself. I pray you, don't turn me into a frog, dear Isabel."

He chuckled again, and she belatedly joined in. While he claimed she was charming, he was the prince of charming. Could someone be too agreeable? Or was she merely viewing him in comparison to the much less charming and affable Adam Driscoll? "You know all about my ancestry, Geoffrey, but I know very little about you. Tell me three things about yourself you wish me to know."

"My favorite topic," he quipped, sitting back a little as their waiter appeared at the side of the table once more.

"Would you care to see a menu, my lord?"

"Not necessary. I will have the pheasant, and Miss de Rossi will have the lamb with mint jelly."

"Very good, my lord."

Geoffrey refilled their glasses himself as the waiter retreated. Isabel hid her frown behind another sip of horrible wine. She would have preferred ordering her own luncheon, and she definitely wouldn't have chosen the lamb, but this only demonstrated how little she knew about proper proceedings. For instance, she'd had no idea that gentlemen selected the meals for the ladies with whom they dined.

"Three things," he mused. "About me, that I wish you to know."

"That I don't already know," she added, hopefully to forestall him from using one or two of his choices to claim how much he liked and admired her.

"Clever minx," he countered in a smooth drawl.

"Thank you," she returned, though she didn't consider what she'd said particularly clever or at all naughty, which was the only reason she could conjure for him calling her a minx. Perhaps, though, she was being naïve again, and all the young ladies in London this year were "chits" and "minxes". She'd heard that first one while out walking with Grandmama Olivia, and no one had seemed put out to hear it.

He flashed that attractive smile again. "Very well. For the first, I adore fishing, and am rather excellent at it if I say so myself. I'm afraid that in my company you shall have to tolerate dining on trout or bass weekly."

"My grandpapa Pietro in Florence has a similar passion," she returned. "We dined on fish often." As for the bit about her being in his company enough to dine on fish weekly, she would put that to his confidence about their joined future. He did make it all rather easy to imagine. Pretty and perfect.

"I'm glad to hear it. I don't think I could marry a woman who couldn't abide *il pesce*," he said, using the Italian word for fish.

"Ah, well done. But I will not be distracted." Not even by the word *marriage*. "What is your second thing?"

"Hmm." For a moment he furrowed his brow, but she suspected his hesitation was for show. He'd just breezed through a conversation that imagined them already married, after all.

Well, staring was rude, so she turned her gaze out the window while he considered which secret he wished to divulge next. Her curricle and pair of matched grays waited just up the road and in plain view, while a steady stream of passersby strolled by. A man dressed as a farmer sent the chickens fleeing as he and a dog drove a half dozen sheep by, a little boy of four or five following and towing a lamb on a rope behind him.

Most of them were her people, and eventually she hoped to learn all of their names, their dreams, their skills, and their needs.

She looked forward to it, to being here at Nimway and having Adam introduce her about. He'd agreed to give her four months of his expertise. She would make certain that was enough. Because asking him to stay longer would be a very bad idea – for both of them.

"I am an only child," the viscount said, drawing her attention back into the inn. "As are you, yes?"

"Yes, I am."

"My father passed seven years ago. My mother resides year-round at my house in London, which is the reason I spend a great deal of my time at Blackbridge and Alton. She's a supremely opinionated woman, I'm afraid, but I've learned to smile and nod and then do as I please. I reckon she'll like you, though, if for no other reason than you domesticating me."

Three footmen arrived with their meal, and while lamb wasn't her favorite she had to acknowledge that it had been prepared quite well. Geoffrey likewise pronounced his pheasant pleasant, a rather obvious attempt at humor, but at least he was making the effort.

Isabel was glad for the lull in conversation. Something about the luncheon felt odd, and she wanted to blame that on Adam. If he hadn't kissed her, if he hadn't tricked her into agreeing to luncheon tomorrow, if he would just leave her thoughts for a blasted minute or two, annoying man, her attention wouldn't be so dreadfully divided. She would simply be listening to and happily chatting with Lord Alton while her life went forward as it should toward a fairy-tale marriage to a very handsome, very charming man who didn't argue with her every time she said the word "magic".

"I confess to some trepidation over telling you the third thing about me," he said, refilling her glass yet again, "because I fear you'll think I'm trying to impress you."

He paused, and she realized she was supposed to say something complimentary in return. Again she wished her education had included a few more lessons in proper conversation with members of the opposite sex. "I trust you to be truthful, Geoffrey, and I'm already quite impressed."

"Well, then. I...have always been fascinated with the legends of Merlin and Arthur, and the search for true magic in the world."

That made her blink. Did he think her a fool, after all? "You've researched magic, then?"

"I've mostly studied tricks – sleight of hand, charming serpents, disappearing objects – but they have left me convinced that there must be something real to balance so much fakery." His light-blue gaze caught and held hers. "Since I've met you, Isabel, I'm more convinced of that than ever. And I'd be willing to wager that you've seen true magic."

She fiddled with her fork for a moment. This wasn't the first time he'd said he believed in magic; technically his confession didn't fulfill the criteria of three things she didn't know about him. But to hear that he'd actually studied the history of magic – that was new. And it actually made her a little...uneasy. It should have left her ecstatic, she supposed, but mainly she heard Adam pointing out that children believed in magic. Adults did not.

This felt different than the magic in which she believed, however. He seemed to be speaking not of the glowing orb sort of magic, but of the objects floating about the room sort. Unless he *was* merely trying to flatter her, and thought he'd deciphered her beliefs.

"Have you?" he prompted.

Isabel blinked. "Have I what?"

"Seen true magic. I can think of no one more likely to have done so."

"Well, we did manage to locate an old orb that's been in the family for generations. A polished moonstone gripped by golden eagle or dragon claws. It's quite lovely, and the legends say it does...something magical on occasion." Yes, she'd seen it glow, but no one else had. And she preferred not to have to prove its abilities when half the time it did nothing at all.

Just why she felt the need to word all that so carefully she had no idea, especially since Geoffrey only greeted her statement with an encouraging smile. It simply made her feel…safer to do so.

"Truly?" he asked, lowering his voice a little. "What have you seen it do? I would love the opportunity to take a look at it, with your permission, of course."

Adam had seen it. For heaven's sake, it had ended up in his bedchamber twice, though she suspected that was because someone was matchmaking. And it hadn't done anything in his presence. "I believe I have seen it glow," she returned.

"Then I *must* see it. Say you'll have me over for dinner, and you can show it off. I promise to be full of admiration."

With a laugh at his eagerness, Isabel brushed aside the nonsense and skepticism Adam had been throwing in her direction. Adults could believe, because magic was real. Him choosing not to do so simply made him obtuse. "That's a fair distance for you to travel just for dinner."

"I don't mind. And there's always business I can attend to in Balesborough. I frequently take a room at the inn here."

The proper thing to do would likely be to invite him to spend the weekend or some such, but she couldn't quite bring herself to do that. Not yet. Not when he was already so certain that a match between them was a foregone conclusion. "If you're certain, then please come to dinner on Saturday. We'll eat early."

Geoffrey inclined his head. "I will admit there are times I wish you had a brother or an uncle or your father commanding your household so I could spend more time there with you. Staying for a week or so would no doubt leave you as convinced as I already am that we are perfectly suited for one another. You know what propriety demands, though, and I reluctantly commend you for protecting your reputation."

Goodness. Propriety hadn't even occurred to her. Another lesson on which they hadn't spent enough time. That didn't mean she couldn't use it to her advantage now that he'd pointed it out, though. "Thank you for understanding, Geoffrey."

"Of course. I'm exceedingly understanding."

After that they chatted about horses and King Arthur's reputed burial site at the old cathedral in Glastonbury and, after she mentioned the sudden appearance of Mist, how his old nursemaid had once sworn she saw a witch turn into a cat. Lord Alton could be quite amusing, and she caught herself laughing several times.

When they finally rose from the table the glimpse she had of his pocket watch showed the time to be nearly three o'clock. Billy waited in the shade beside the curricle, rising to climb onto the seat as she and Geoffrey approached.

"I shall count the hours until Saturday, you know," the viscount said, stopping to face her as he took both of her hands in both of his. "It shall be a sweet torture." Lowering his head, he lifted her hands and kissed each of her knuckles before he straightened again.

"Thank you again for luncheon," she returned. "It, and the company, were delightful."

He handed her up beside Billy. "I shall see you in three days, dear Isabel." With that he sketched a bow, doffing his hat as he did so, then turned to collect his bay stallion.

"I'm sorry to be so long, Billy," she said, as the groom clucked at the team and sent them off at a trot. "I had no idea of the time."

"Not to worry, Miss Isabel," he returned with an easy grin. "I had myself a fine nap, and the stalls will have been mucked out hours ago. You'll hear no complaining from Billy Barnes."

She had no complaints, either. Just a few nagging worries over whether a man could be too perfect. And over what the other, much less perfect man in her life would say when he learned she'd invited Lord Alton for dinner on Saturday. And over whether the orb would finally stop being so stubborn and let her know that it agreed with her about Geoffrey.

Because she had the sneaking suspicion that the orb – or someone who knew both where it had been and where she was hiding it now – had a different fellow in mind. And she was certain she didn't agree with that at all. Fairly certain, anyway.

CHAPTER 12

*W*ell, at least Adam hadn't decided to take her to the Two-Headed Dragon for luncheon. As he drove the curricle deeper into the Balesboro Wood, Isabel wasn't certain, in fact, if he had any idea at all where they *were* going.

"We already inspected the logging hut," she offered, ducking beneath a branch as they continued along a rapidly fading path.

"I recall. The hut's farther west of here."

She sent him a sideways glance, but all his attention appeared to be on the overgrown track and the pair of grays. "I think this might be a deer trail."

"That is very likely."

They continued on as the track meandered downhill, until it stopped before an old tree that had fallen squarely across the path. It was covered in moss, with mushrooms peeking out of the undergrowth of ferns that had sprouted along its length. "We seem to have reached the end of the trail," she observed. "Do we go back?"

Adam tied off the leads and hopped to the ground. "We walk," he said, coming around to her side of the curricle.

"I'm not wearing appropriate shoes for clambering through

the forest, you know." Nevertheless, she stood. Whatever he was up to, it was unexpected. And she found that very intriguing.

Before she could climb down from the carriage, Adam put his hands around her waist and lifted her to the forest floor. The ground beneath her feet was uneven, and she grabbed onto his arms to keep her balance. Given the ease with which he'd lifted her, she wouldn't have been surprised to see him lift the curricle, horses and all, over the fallen log. Instead, he kept his splayed hands on her waist until she lifted her head to look up at him.

"It's not far," he said, and took her left hand in his right. "This way."

"What isn't far?" she asked, hiking up her skirt with her free hand and following him around the tree and down a slight incline. "Certain death?"

He chuckled. "That's in the other direction."

"Oh, good." Holding hands might not be proper, but his warm, firm grip kept her from falling on her face at least twice. And it made her feel...safe, despite the setting.

She'd already noted that he hadn't loaded a picnic basket or even a blanket onto the curricle, and he certainly wasn't carrying one with him now. Hopefully he had an apple or two in his pockets, or they would stumble across some wild whortleberries, because she was quite hungry. Perhaps she'd been more nervous about today's luncheon than she'd admitted to herself, because she'd barely managed a piece of toast for breakfast, and that had been hours ago.

They'd walked less than a minute beyond the fallen tree when he stopped. "We're here."

Isabel looked around. Trees, shrubberies, ferns, and a thick tangle of brambles directly before them. Beyond the breeze rustling through the leaves and the scattering of birdsongs, she could make out the sound of flowing water somewhere close by, but no stream lay in sight. "Are you certain of that?"

By way of answer he pulled the brambles aside and motioned her forward. "You'll have to duck a little."

Well, she'd come this far. Isabel ducked beneath the archway he'd made and stepped forward, keeping her gaze on the ground so she wouldn't trip. Seeing grass beneath her feet, she looked up. And gasped.

Old, old trees and brambles formed a half wall around a small glade, the other half bounded by a steep, rocky hillside. In the center, white roses climbed the trunk of an absolutely ancient-looking oak tree. To one side of the tree, a small waterfall cascaded into a pond, while beyond it a trio of large white boulders crouched in the grass. On this side of the pond a blue blanket had been laid out, together with a generous-sized basket.

"This… How did you find this place?" she asked, facing Adam as he ducked beneath the brambles to join her.

"Last month I was tracing the stream back and nearly fell into the pond. The boulders have faces carved into them. From sometime before the Romans were here, I would guess."

She traipsed through the grass and meadow flowers to the nearest of the white stones. It took some squinting, but after a moment she made out two large eyes, a very generous nose, and a straight mouth above a beard that carried on down into the earth. Her breath stopped. Could this be some sculptor's depiction of Merlin himself? She ran her fingers along the worn edges.

"Not as fine as your father's work," Adam noted, crouching beside her, "but striking all the same."

"It's extraordinary," she breathed. "Thank you for showing me."

"It's yours. I'm not an expert in naming things by any means, as you know, but I thought you might consider calling this place Isabel's Bower."

Oh, she liked that. Smiling, she straightened to go look at the other two white boulders. A supremely buxom woman graced one of them, while some sort of maned leopard or spotted lion with eagle's feet decorated the third. The claws very much reminded her of the orb's golden claws holding the moonstone in place. "I want to do rubbings of these," she said, tracing the lion-leopard's tail with her fingertips.

"Perhaps in fabric," he suggested. "You could have them framed."

"You're being unexpectedly imaginative," she said, straightening again.

"Not believing in dancing fairies doesn't make me unimaginative," he returned, walking back to the blanket. "In fact, you have no idea some of the things I'm imagining at this very moment. They do involve you, by the way."

Heat trailed beneath her skin. "I stand corrected," she said, unable to help wondering precisely what he was imagining. Given his direct gaze and the way he'd spoken, no doubt it was something terribly improper.

"Good." He seated himself, folding his long legs and untying the lid of the basket. "Now. I wasn't sure what you'd like, but I spoke with Mrs. Dall and she assured me that either shepherd's pie or cucumber- and mutton-sandwiches or something with tomatoes and bread that she couldn't quite describe to me but that you ate in Florence would suffice. We had no tomatoes, but she managed the other two."

With a flourish he removed a cloth-covered plate of sandwiches and a deep dish of shepherd's pie from the basket. Then he set out plates, utensils, and glasses, together with a bowl of sugared strawberries and a bottle of Madeira.

"You didn't have to bring both," she said, sitting on the far side of the blanket and settling her white-and-brown skirts around her.

"Yes, I did. Neither Mrs. Dall nor I knew which meal you preferred. I'm attempting to woo you, in case you've forgotten."

The flutter of her heart, the tingling at the tips of her fingers, resumed again. He barely qualified as a gentleman, she supposed, but he certainly provided her with an additional perspective regarding luncheon etiquette, anyway. She was permitted to choose her own meal, apparently. "I haven't forgotten."

"Sandwiches, or shepherd's pie, then?"

"Sandwiches."

He served them to her, then settled onto one elbow with his own. "Is the orb still where you placed it?" he asked. "I've taken to checking beneath my pillow, but it hasn't reappeared."

"You're making fun of me now."

Adam lifted an eyebrow. "I am not. It's been on my windowsill and on my dressing table. Beneath the pillow could well be next."

She needed to remind herself that not everything he said was meant to begin an argument. Just nearly everything. "I checked it this morning," she said. "As of then it was still safe." Actually she hadn't so much checked on it as she had shaken the thing half to death while cajoling it to give her some sign that Geoffrey Bell-Spratt was her true love. Perhaps she'd broken the orb after all, because it hadn't even glowed when she'd picked it up.

"Will your parents or your grandparents visit you here?" he went on, leaning sideways to offer her a strawberry. "With you just stepping into your position, I can't imagine you wanting to leave long enough to travel to Florence."

"Mama and Papa have promised to come for Christmas," she returned. "They actually offered to travel here with me. I asked them not to. How would I know if I can be the guardian here with either my mother or Grandmama Olivia present?"

"That was brave."

She couldn't mistake the sincerity of those three words. He wasn't being sarcastic, or condescending. He meant it, and as a compliment. She lifted her shoulder a little. "Thank you. A large portion of it was naivety though, I think. I half expected mystical warriors and swords rising out of lakes. That was foolish."

Adam tilted his head. "Whatever you expected, you're taking steps to learn how to manage an estate. In all the world where status is inherited, you certainly weren't alone in being unprepared. But you haven't been satisfied with remaining that way. And that's commendable."

Isabel smiled at him. She wasn't accustomed to voicing her inner doubts aloud, and he might have used them to skewer her pride and her sense of accomplishment at what she'd learned thus far. But he hadn't done so. And he hadn't turned it into a jest, or made a comment about his superior abilities in comparison to hers. "You're full of compliments this afternoon. I'm more accustomed to arguments from you."

He sent her a swift grin. "Differences of opinion, perhaps. And I've been told that arguing connotes passion."

"And who told you that?"

"My father, when I wrote him last week."

Oh, this was becoming very interesting, indeed. She popped a strawberry into her mouth, noting that he watched her every move. It felt...powerful to realize he had so much of his attention focused on her. She hadn't felt that way in Geoffrey's presence – but then they'd been dining in public, where every nuance would be noticed and speculated over. And besides, she didn't want to think about that right now. This was merely a pleasant luncheon. "May I ask what else you discussed? And what prompted your letter?"

"Some of it was private, asking after my mother's health. She's been ill, but they went to Bath for her to take the waters, and she feels much recovered. Mainly, I wrote to say that I'd met an impossible female whose view of the most basic facts of the world was completely at odds with mine."

"Ah. Do I know this female?"

"Quite well. I said that I respected her intelligence and her wit and the interest she's taken in learning her duties and responsibilities, but that we argued about everything else."

It was odd to realize that she liked the way Adam Driscoll viewed her. Even with his criticism and skepticism over her beliefs, he seemed genuinely to respect and admire her. He had never brushed aside her questions or attempted to turn her aside with humor or faux self-deprecation. And no, she didn't wish to think about whom else she might be describing. "And that was what prompted his observation about arguing."

"Yes. And in response to my question about whether I could continue to work for this female given her very singular view of the world, he said, and I'm quoting because I memorized it, 'Ask yourself two questions. Firstly, if you can live *with* those opposing beliefs and secondly, if you can live *without* this impossible female'."

Goodness. Beneath everything else, he'd written his father for advice about her. Isabel cleared her throat. "And have you found an answer to those questions?"

Green eyes held hers. "Very nearly."

"Oh." She shifted a little, hoping he didn't notice that she felt as awkward as her eight-year-old tiara-wearing self, or that he would ever suspect that she'd once or twice imagined him in knight's armor as he rode up on a great white charger to bring her flowers. Trying to shake loose of that image, she sought about for something that wouldn't leave her gaping like a moonstruck goose. "Perhaps I could tolerate becoming better acquainted with you. Tell me three things about you that you want me to know. Three things I don't already know."

Adam lifted an eyebrow. "What? No," he said around a mouthful of sandwich.

"Why shouldn't you tell me about yourself?" she demanded. It had been supremely enlightening with Lord Alton.

"You already know about me, Isabel. And why would you settle for three things, anyway? You know I'm pursuing you, so I would only choose things you would look on favorably." He sat upright again. "Did you put this challenge to Alton?" Adam snorted. "You did, didn't you? Did you discover you have, oh, so many things in common? That he simply can't resist small animals in distress?"

Well, animals hadn't been mentioned, but that was beside the point. And he was more right than she cared to admit. Was she so easily swayed? "Your being pleasant didn't last for very long," she said aloud. "I was wondering when the compliments would stop."

To her surprise he laughed, though his expression remained rather grim. "So you want me to begin agreeing with you at every instance? Just follow along behind you like some yapping dog?"

"You don't have to agree with me. You could be agreeable more often, though."

"I am frequently agreeable, and you are perfectly aware of that fact. I've also promised to be honest with you. Always." Abruptly he shifted onto his knees, then went forward onto all fours, putting his face just inches from hers. "I have never once lied to you," he continued more softly, "not even to make you see me more favorably." He tilted his head a little. "Generally in a romantic pursuit, it is the man who leads, who holds all the cards, as it were. You're my employer, and you own a magnificent property. All I have to offer you, then, is myself and my good name. And my heart, of course."

A kiss. He was going to kiss her again. The fast beat of her pulse thudded in her chest all the way out to her fingertips. When he kissed her, everything made sense – or at least she managed to forget for a moment everything that didn't.

"I am, as they say, a sure bet, Isabel," he murmured. "If and when you decide what and who you want, I shall be here." He looked at her in silence for a handful of ragged heartbeats. "Until our contract is up, that is. Because I'm not a yapping dog, and I will not wait forever." With a faint grin, as if he knew precisely what he did to her insides, he picked up another sandwich, sat back, and took a bite.

Isabel blinked. Yes, she knew they'd arranged for him to remain at Nimway for four months, and that they'd made the agreement after he'd rather spectacularly kissed her that first time. It hardly seemed likely that he'd had all this in mind then, that he knew he wanted to marry her and that four months would be sufficient to bring her around to his way of thinking. And feeling.

"You're done with wooing then?" she ventured, deciding she should say something, and trying not to sound disappointed that there wouldn't be kissing today. "You've stated your position and now it's up to me to decide?"

He reached out to brush a finger along her cheek. "I can't and won't coerce you into liking me. But if this isn't wooing, perhaps I'm doing it wrong after all."

"Of course you're doing it wrong. You make light of something I deeply believe, and write your father to say you like me in spite of my naïve stupidity? My stupid naïveté? Geoffrey Bell-Spratt likes me as well, and he actually believes me. He even believes in magic. Why, then, would I choose you?"

"I would suggest you ask him in front of his cronies if he believes in magic," Adam snapped. Standing, he left the picnic blanket and strode over to the stream. "I could tell you that I believe. Would you like me better for paying you lip service, or worse for lying in order to impress you?"

As he spoke, sun broke through the thick canopy above them, the shafts of light visible streaks illuminating two of the white carved stones...and Adam. The white of his simple cravat glinted like fresh snow, the green of his eyes as he glared at her becoming a bottomless emerald. As she stared at the only Sir Galahad who didn't believe in the Holy Grail, clouds slowly moved in again, dimming the boulders but causing the sunlight to linger on him for several more seconds before it faded again.

"Which is it?" he prompted.

If the world was trying to tell her something, she had a large disagreement with it. "I would very nearly be satisfied if you would just accept the possibility of something beyond what you can touch with your stupid hands," she retorted, and threw a strawberry at the infuriating man.

Adam caught the treat in one hand and popped it into his mouth. It was likely fortunate that he'd spent most of his adult life settling disputes between neighbors and finding solutions for impossible problems. That at least gave him the insight to recognize that as frustrated as he was that Isabel wouldn't see Alton for who he was, or the world for what it was, she was just as frustrated with him for not seeing things as she did.

Had he backed himself into a corner with his insistence on being a gentleman? If he merely pretended to be one, though, he might as well have been Alton. "I brought lemon biscuits, unless you'd prefer we return to the house now," he said, returning to sit on the blanket.

"You...are very aggravating. Did Mrs. Dall bake the biscuits?"

"Yes."

"Biscuits, then. But I'm not certain I wish to continue conversing with you."

He dug back into the basket and uncovered the plate. "While we're not speaking," he said, offering her the treats, "from where does the money come that Alton uses to pay his staff and his taxes at Blackbridge or Alton Park?"

"What?"

"You have your crops and your timber rights. What do his estates produce? He dresses well and rides a horse with twelve names. I assume he affords this somehow."

"I assume so, as well. The conversation hasn't come up."

"I'd wager he knows where your money comes from. You mean income wasn't one of the three things he told you about himself?"

She frowned around the biscuit. "He didn't ask me to luncheon to discuss finances."

Adam had to give the viscount some credit; whatever he'd told Isabel had convinced her that they would suit well. "Ah. Then you talked about where you mean to live after he wins your hand. It will be Blackbridge, I assume, since that estate's merely a two-hour ride from Nimway Park."

"You have nowhere else to go, though, do you?"

He looked at her. "No. I wasn't born first, or with an estate just waiting for me to be old enough to claim it. I could purchase a small farm somewhere, or an apartment in London, I suppose, if I wished to."

Her fine cheeks paled a little. "I didn't mean to insult you. I just meant—"

"You have a beautiful estate, Isabel," he broke in. "I like it here. I like working here, and I like working with you. For you, even.

And I know you look for the magic in everything. You see the best in everyone. That's one of the things I lo— admire about you." He took a breath. He'd very nearly admitted that he'd fallen in love with her – which he had, but confessing to it now would smack of weakness. Of pleading.

"Alton has his own concerns," he pressed. "His own properties. I have…this. Here." However she felt about him, she would have to acknowledge the logic and practicality of that, at least. "The moment I arrived at Nimway, I could imagine being here forever."

"For four months," she countered. "You agreed to that, if you'll recall."

"I'll take whatever I can get," he said, unable to help the…anger, he supposed it was, at the idea that he would have to leave Nimway. Especially when Alton seemed to have an invitation to remain. "Just – for God's sake don't ignore the practicality of people's desires, wants, and needs," he pressed. "Alton has his own properties that require his attention. You know that. Before you agree to anything, ask yourself what Alton wants here, and *why* he wants it. Ask why *I* want what I want. Then do what you can to figure out if what you're being told is the truth."

"If you're too gentlemanly to tell me what you clearly think you know about Geoffrey, then you should stop hurling ominous, vague warnings about him." With that she brushed off her skirt. "And now I would like to return home."

God, he wanted to tell her. Every damned bit of it. But he honestly didn't know the viscount's side of the tale. And it had been nearly six years. People did change. He could hardly blame Alton for falling for Isabel, and in fact he couldn't be entirely certain how much of his present venom was due to the fact that he wanted Isabel de Rossi for himself.

"As you wish," he said aloud, and stood once more. He held down a hand to help her to her feet, trying to ignore the hard thud of his pulse as their fingers touched. He offered his arm, but she fairly obviously pretended not to notice as she stalked toward the wall of brambles.

Snagging one more of the crisp biscuits and chomping into it, Adam followed her. Only part of his father's letter had directly concerned Adam's own confusion of feelings about Isabel. The rest had also been about her, but in regard to Alton's courtship. The old baron had pointed out that while the Driscoll family carried their own well-earned prejudices against the viscount, they were also personal prejudices, colored by their personal views. And it would be unfair to Isabel and to the viscount to apply them to the rest of the world.

"What about the basket and blanket?" Isabel asked abruptly, facing him.

He shrugged, finishing off the biscuit. "I brought them earlier. I'll come get them later."

"Nonsense. We're here now. I may be annoyed with you, but I don't expect you to make an extra trip to appease my temper." She stomped past him, heading back toward the picnic blanket.

Utterly unpredictable. "But you wanted to go back to the house." Stifling an admiring grin, he turned around to catch up to her again.

"Well, despite your unending stubbornness this was very... thoughtful of you."

"'Thoughtful'. A fairly weak compliment, but thank you for it."

"You're somewhat welcome." What might have been a smile twitched at the corner of her mouth as she knelt on the blanket, picking up plates and bowls and placing them carefully back into the basket.

Adam squatted beside her, helping himself to another biscuit as they packed up the remains of luncheon. This impossible woman aggravated the devil out of him, but at the same time he couldn't help but admire her more every day.

"The clouds are building," he observed, looking at the leaf-obscured sky above them. "We'll have rain by midnight."

Isabel stood again, hands on her hips, to glare down at him. "You are a man of common sense and commendable character.

143

No one told me this. I know it from seeing what you do every day and how you talk to people."

He straightened, but she didn't back away even though he was the one who now loomed over her. "I assume you're not suddenly bursting with the need to compliment me," he returned. "What point are you after, then?"

"I'm after an answer," she retorted. "Are you simply…jealous of Lord Alton because I enjoy his company? Or is there something I truly need to know? I demand an answer!"

"Of course I'm jealous," he snapped, drawing in a hard breath. "As for him, you—" Adam clenched his fist, unable to stifle a growl. "I told you my opinion that no one matters to Alton as much as he matters to himself. Perhaps that's acceptable to you. I don't know. Is he a criminal? Not that I'm aware of. Just…listen to him when he speaks, because at the time I last encountered him I learned that he does nothing that isn't to his own benefit. Nothing. If he's changed, huzzah, but I will continue trying to win your affection, anyway."

Her hands stayed on her hips, but her glare became a frustrated grimace. Those lips twisted, and he took a half step forward before he could stop himself. How could it be coercion if he simply pulled her into his arms and kissed her again? Of course she'd more than likely slap him, but he'd never been averse to risk.

"Adam, just tell me."

He tilted his head. "You need to make your own decision. The wrong he did me was personal and moral, and nothing I could prove even if I wished to. Ask him. But I doubt you'll get an answer from Alton, either."

Isabel sighed. "He's already called you a small, jealous man, and said you misinterpret everything in order to keep yourself blameless. But I'll ask him again when he comes to Nimway Hall on Saturday for dinner."

The words were rushed, and as his comprehension caught up to what she'd said, he realized why she'd been in a hurry to spit them out. *The bastard.* "Did you invite him, or did he invite himself?" he ground out.

"I told him about the orb, and he wanted to see it. Hence the invitation." Isabel put an unexpected palm over his heart. That touch was all that kept him from stalking out of the bower, himself.

At least they were speaking again. "You want the orb to see him."

"Yes, I do."

"And what if your magic orb tells you one thing, and your heart another?"

"I thought you didn't believe in such things."

"*I* don't. *You* do. Though I don't require an orb to tell me who to care for." Adam put his hand over hers where it covered his chest.

"You called me an impossible woman," she said, gray eyes as deep as the sea. "I'm afraid I must likewise declare you an impossible man."

He smiled, the bindings holding his heart tethered breaking loose when her sweet lips curved to match his expression. Adam leaned in – and stopped when she put her free hand over his mouth.

"If you kiss me now," she whispered, "I'll never be able to figure this out."

Adam supposed if she shifted her affections to match the direction of the wind or simpered and flirted and didn't care to be serious about any of this, he wouldn't have felt as drawn to her as he did. That didn't make it less maddening. He *knew*. He was willing to overlook her silly fascination with magic. Isabel, though, didn't seem to wish to overlook his doubts.

He kissed her palm before wrapping his fingers about her wrist to pull it away. "It goes against every instinct I possess to simply stand aside and wait," he said. "But you've clearly convinced yourself that you don't need to make a decision with your heart because the orb will do it for you." He stepped away from her and bent down to pick up the blanket, shake it out, and fold it.

"That's not fair, Adam."

It didn't please him, either. With a noncommittal grunt he shoved the blanket through the basket's handle, then picked the whole thing up. "Shall we?" he said, and offered his arm again.

Still scowling at him, she grabbed hold as they ducked through the brambles and picked their way back to the curricle. In two days the enemy would be not just at the gates, but inside the house. Not his house, but nevertheless one of which he'd grown supremely fond. And one that was under his protection.

Alton would do whatever he could to convince Isabel that her blasted orb had chosen him. For once Adam wished he could lower himself to do the same. Or at least to wish that the magic it supposedly possessed, and that she believed in so strongly, was real.

Because he knew down to his bones that Isabel belonged with him. It was only his ability to convince her that concerned him. Worried him. Terrified him.

CHAPTER 13

*I*sabel lay on her stomach, chin on her folded arms, and stared at the orb in its golden-clawed base just beyond the end of her nose. "Glow," she muttered. "Show me a face. Shine a beam of light. You're meant to help me."

Nothing. She freed one arm and tapped the moonstone with her forefinger. It wobbled, then righted itself again. Pursing her lips, she blew on it.

"Are you angry because I hid you in my riding boot? I would put you on display if I knew how and why you kept disappearing. I'm trying to keep you safe."

It remained where it was, doing nothing. Just as it had done nothing since she'd retrieved it from Adam's bedchamber the second time. With a sigh she caught hold of it and sat upright. How disappointing if the orb had used up the last of its magic. Without it, would Nimway Hall still be…itself? What would she pass on to her oldest daughter – if she could tear herself away from dreams of Adam in favor of the much more sophisticated Geoffrey? The property, of course, but not only did Nimway mean acreage, it was myth and legend and promise. And magic.

And if the orb still held magic, why wasn't she worthy enough to see it? To have it help her choose the path of her life? After all, she had one man who also cared about Nimway but who refused to see its heart. And she had another man who believed as she did, who was charming and flattering and who wanted to give her a fairy-tale life, but who left her wondering how much time she would be able actually to spend at Nimway Hall.

Jane knocked on the door. "Isabel?"

"I'm still in here."

Her companion pushed open the door and practically bounced into the room. "He's just crested the rise," she announced. "Not five minutes away, now."

Of course "he" would be Geoffrey Bell-Spratt. Giving the orb a last, warning shake, she wrapped it in her dark-blue scarf and tucked it against her elbow. "Then let's go say hello, shall we?"

"Are you certain you want an old spinster like me to join you? You'll have Simmons and the footmen there to keep everything proper."

"You're part of my family, Jane. If you and he don't get on well, he's not the man for me." Isabel joined her companion at the door. "And with the orb not doing anything, I am relying on your assessment of his character."

"Very well, but it's entirely possible I'll become lost in his gorgeous blue eyes and not pay attention to anything else."

Isabel snorted. "Then we can both be lost together." The orb bumped against her arm, and she tightened her grip on it. She'd said she would show it to Geoffrey, and with its tendency to vanish she wasn't taking any chances.

"I just hope Mr. Driscoll doesn't decide to wander by while Lord Alton is here. You said they don't get along."

They headed down the hallway together. "No, they do not, though neither of them will bother to tell me why. But I informed Adam that I would be entertaining tonight, and with whom. And I instructed Simmons to have Mr. Driscoll's dinner brought to his bedchamber. I'm not taking any chances."

"This is very exciting. I hope the orb does glow or spin or

whatever it's going to do. Then we'll have a wedding, and your parents and grandparents will come, then you'll have a daughter, and she'll have your birthmark as well, and Nimway Hall will have its next guardian. And it all begins tonight!"

A shiver of unease ran down Isabel's spine. Her entire future, laid out in one sentence. What if the first step, the orb, failed? Did that mean her ancestors didn't or wouldn't approve any match? That they didn't approve of her? Would she be the last guardian?

"Isabel? We need to go downstairs, my dear."

Her hand clenched the stair railing, and she was most definitely not moving. Isabel shook herself. "Of course. A stray thought caught hold of me."

"A good thought, I hope?"

"How could it be otherwise?" Forcing a smile, she continued down to the foyer.

Discounting her anxiety over tonight's dinner, she actually did have several reasons to be thinking happy thoughts. The bees had two actual hives now, and the honey Mr. Hayward had showed them how to extract from the chest of drawers had graced her toasted bread this morning. A half dozen orange trees had arrived, and so had Mr. Hodgins, giving her hope that the orangery would be finished before the cold weather set in. Top Drawer Honey could be selling its first jars by the end of next spring.

Adam had given her his calendar, and she'd begun making notations of her own to remind her what needed to be seen to and when to do it. Initially all the tasks, and the variety of them, had felt chaotic and overwhelming, and whenever a new task appeared she had to quash the instant feeling that she wouldn't be up to managing it.

To her great surprise, though, she'd begun to discover that life at Nimway Hall had a rhythm to it. A heartbeat, almost. And slowly, very slowly, she felt as though she could feel its pulse. For that, she could thank Adam.

Oh, he was so close to being a perfect match for her. There were times over the past few days she'd been able to forget for minutes at a time that he – an employee – had never once hesitated to tell her that she was wrong about something. In fact, he seemed to take a particular kind of delight in arguing with her. And in claiming that his opinion had more merit than hers because it was based in logic rather than instinct and things she simply *knew* to be true.

Simmons opened the front door, and she tried to shake herself free of Adam, of remembering that he was equally generous with praise when she performed her new duties up to his standards. Before she even had time to take a last, deep breath, Viscount Alton strolled into the foyer. Swiftly he handed the butler his hat and coat. That done, he walked up, took her free hand, and bowed over it.

"It seems like weeks since I last set eyes on you, Isabel," he stated, brushing his lips against her knuckles. "You are a vision."

Now *that* was how a gentleman should greet a lady. It pleased her that he'd noticed the mauve-and-black silk gown she'd donned; she and her mother and Jane had gone to Paris themselves to order it. She curtsied as well as she could with one hand captured and the other holding the well-wrapped orb. "Thank you, Geoffrey."

His gaze lowered to the bundle in her arms. "Is that it? May I see it?"

"Let's repair to the drawing room, shall we? I'll show it to you while we wait for dinner."

"Certainly. Lead the way."

He trailed Jane and her up the stairs, but paused every few feet to praise something else he'd noticed about Nimway Hall. The cornices were magnificent. The foyer chandelier was exquisite, of a crystal that most houses couldn't afford. The stairway bannisters were of the finest mahogany he'd ever seen, and the price of mahogany was outrageous these days. A frown furrowed her brow, but she swiftly banished it again. There was nothing wrong with seeing the beauty in things. And if he'd used as fine a compliment on the curtains as he had on her gown, well, that was merely his way of expressing himself. As for his knowledge of what the bits and bobs of Nimway were worth, perhaps it was just another foible. None of Nimway was for sale, after all.

"I tried to find a record of when, precisely, Nimway Hall was built, to give me some insight into its architecture," he said, as she led the way into the drawing room.

"What did you discover?"

"I discovered that if there are records somewhere, I can't find them. All I can say with any certainty is that there's been a house on this spot, in one form or another, for a very long time." He turned in a slow circle. "A very long time."

"I could have told you that," Isabel returned, smiling. As she spoke, though, Adam's warnings about Geoffrey and his motivations began swirling through her mind. She didn't want them to be there, because she preferred being able to take people at their word. She wasn't gullible – or at least she thought not – but since she knew Adam Driscoll to be an honest man, it would be stupid and naïve on her part to disregard his warnings. Especially with the orb not giving her any clue yet which way to turn.

"We *have* been here for ages, Geoffrey, even if our surnames change with each generation, because that is what happens when a property passes down the female line. Why are you so interested in our architecture now?"

The viscount faced her straight on, his expression the typical one of mild amusement. "You sounded like a true guardian of Nimway Hall just then, speaking through the ages. It gave me goosebumps."

And that had been a fine compliment. "Thank you."

He held out one hand. "May I see the orb now?"

Abruptly Isabel wanted another moment or two, a few more seconds to think and to breathe. For heaven's sake, her fate rested on all of this. Or at the least, her future. She squared her shoulders. In essence she'd been waiting for this moment for eighteen years. And that was long enough.

Looking down, she removed the blue scarf from around the

old orb. Keeping her fingers from touching it to avoid influencing anything, she held it out to Geoffrey.

With his attention seemingly divided between the orb and her, the viscount lifted it out of its blue nest. "It's exquisite," he mused, holding it toward the nearest lamp.

The stupid thing didn't glow, but then it hadn't been doing that for the past few days. Still she kept a close eye on it, because if there was ever a time for the orb to do something magical, it was now.

"You said it glowed when you touched it?"

"Yes." More or less, anyway.

"Well. I'm not seeing…" The viscount trailed off, his expression folding into an attractive frown. He didn't seem to own an expression that *wasn't* attractive.

"What is it?" Isabel asked.

"It feels… That is, the moonstone feels warm."

"Well, you're holding it."

He nodded, his frown deepening. "Yes, but…" He shifted one hand, touching the golden claws. "The stone is warm. The gold enclosing it is not. I'm sure of it. In fact, it's quite warm, but not intolerably so." His mouth curved in a surprised smile. "Remarkable. I feel…content. Happy. Like I'm precisely where I'm supposed to be."

Hmm. Perhaps the glowing had just been an acknowledgment of her, and she'd misunderstood what that meant. She'd never really held it long enough to determine whether it emitted heat; she'd been too occupied with poking it and shaking it. "Let me feel it."

Geoffrey started to hold it out to her, then pulled it back again. "I think… Yes, it's cooling." Blue eyes caught hers. "I could never have imagined. Thank you for sharing it with me, Isabel."

When she took it back the stone felt only slightly warm, but he'd admitted that the heat had begun to fade. Was that the sign, then? Had the orb spoken? It didn't feel…special enough, momentous enough for something that meant so much to her future. And yet the orb had reacted when he touched it, which was more than it had done for her since the first time she'd held it.

He still gazed at her. "This is significant, then?"

Across the room Jane cleared her throat before she conspicuously turned away to gaze out the darkened window. That was as private as dinner this evening would get.

"Ah," he said quietly, clearly reading the situation. Lowering his chin he took a long step forward, removed the orb and scarf from her hand to set them on a side table, and slid his arms around her waist.

She closed her eyes as his lips touched hers, anticipating that lifting feeling, as if on the inside she were weightless, jumping down from a very high tree. His slightly damp mouth pressed more firmly against hers, and his tongue pushed between them and bumped against her teeth and her tongue. Her insides stayed just where they were, behind the ribs that he was now squeezing with his palms.

Stifling a scowl, Isabel put a hand on his shoulders and rose up on her toes to kiss him more deeply. His breath smelled of cigars and, try as she might, she couldn't...soar. But he was perfect. The orb certainly thought so. This was stupid Adam's fault. He kissed far more proficiently than he had a right to do. Without his kisses lingering in her thoughts, she would be feeling those butterflies, the lightning coursing up her spine to her fingertips.

Behind her something thudded to the floor. Oh, no – the orb? If she'd broken it now, then she'd still managed to muck up the future for her descendants. Breaking the kiss, she turned around. The scarf remained on the side table, but the orb was most definitely not with it.

"Oh, no," she breathed, sinking onto her hands and knees to look under the table, the couch, and the nearest chair. Nothing. "Help me find the orb!"

Jane gasped and for some reason decided to look behind the window curtains on the far side of the room. Then again, there was no telling where it might have gone.

"I'll check beneath the couch cushions," Geoffrey announced, and began turning over pillows.

Isabel risked a sideways glance at the viscount as they searched. He wore the same mildly amused expression he seemed to spend most of his time showing the world, eyebrows slightly arched, mouth slightly curved – the pleasant look that she found most handsome.

It shouldn't have bothered her to see it now, but it did. If he knew as much about local legends as he claimed, he knew what the orb meant. And he'd kissed her, knowing it was the first kiss of many they would share. Yet there he was, doing a fairly poor job of searching, and wearing the same expression he'd had when they'd been at the mill, when they'd gone walking in East Pennard, and when they'd dined at the Two-Headed Dragon.

If the kiss had pleased him, she couldn't tell. If it had been the worst first kiss ever, she couldn't tell. Congenial was one thing, but where was his passion?

"Miss Isa… Oh, there you are," Simmons said, as he entered the drawing room and found her crouched low on the floor. "Dinner is served."

She caught hold of the back of the couch and pulled herself upright. "Well, this isn't the first time the orb has vanished," she said, settling her skirt and hiding her frown. This man wasn't just a guest, and she couldn't spend the evening crawling about on the floor. Something momentous had happened, and now that she had what she'd wished for, she couldn't quite help wondering whether a mistake had happened, after all.

"Simmons," she said, "the orb fell off the table here, and it seems to have gone missing again."

"I'll send James and Franklin in to scour the corners," the butler said dryly, holding open the door dividing the drawing room from the dining room.

"Thank you," she returned, grimacing as she took a last look at the floor. Where the devil had it gone? But then Geoffrey took her hand and placed it over his arm, practically towing her into the dining room.

Although Lord Alton outranked her this was *her* home, and so Isabel took the seat at the head of the table. Generally Adam sat at her right elbow, and for a moment it felt odd to have another man seated there. But she'd asked this one over because she'd wanted a question answered. Now that it had been answered, however, she abruptly wasn't at all certain she agreed.

"Tell me," Geoffrey said, as the footman brought around a delicious-smelling fish-and-leek soup, "how did your ancestors manage to keep such a profitable property with the female line? If there's no daughter, does it pass to an aunt or a female cousin?"

"Yes, it does. There have been occasions when that was necessary. As for how they managed it, I'm not certain. It's always been that way. I believe it's been contested in the courts more than once by jealous male relations, but to no avail."

"And the only magic here is the orb, choosing husbands for guardians of Nimway Hall through the generations?"

"The orb isn't always necessary, and so it doesn't always appear. And no, it's not the only magic here."

"What else have you seen, then?"

Isabel took two sips of soup as she considered the question, and her answer. Beautiful, sparkling sunrises, a cat who'd appeared from nowhere and now seemed to come and go at will, the deep, satisfying sense of belonging she'd found the moment she'd set foot inside the house – did any of those things provide proof of magic? "I've on occasion heard music, lutes and drums, when no one else was about," she said slowly. "And a sound like chanting, in a language I've never heard before." There. That sounded more magical than some of the things Adam would have dismissed as coincidence.

"Fascinating. And you said the orb had disappeared and reappeared several times as well, yes?"

"Yes. I believe that may be what happened just a moment ago, in fact, and there have been other things. Some may call them luck or fortune, but I prefer to believe that magic…helped them along."

He smiled at her over his glass of wine. "I admit I was hoping for fairies and goblins and flaming swords."

"There isn't much use for flaming swords these days in Somerset," she returned, smiling. He was charming, after all. Perhaps she just needed to look again. To stop making it all fit into her vision instead of just allowing events to unfold as they would.

"I don't know about that. I could think of a few uses for one. Deterring pesky solicitors and other unwanted intruders, for example."

That was supposed to be amusing, even if she did have a very strong feeling that he was referring to Adam. She therefore mustered a chuckle and a nod at his wit before she returned her gaze, if not her attention, to the soup. Everything had just fallen into place. Why, then, was uneasiness slowly creeping up her spine, an odd dread instead of what should have been excitement?

The orb had warmed to his touch; just because it had then disappeared didn't mean anything. It disappeared on a fairly regular basis. This…this was what was supposed to happen. Isabel sent another glance at Geoffrey, who seemed to be enjoying his soup.

He hadn't asked for her hand yet, and they were still two new friends becoming better acquainted. She could ask him questions. She should be asking him questions. "Nimway Hall has our timber rights, our wheat, and our cattle," she said aloud. "What do you produce at Blackbridge and Alton?"

"We produce Bells," he returned, sitting back as the servants collected their soup bowls. "And most recently me, a Bell-Spratt, just to continue the lines of money flow and inheritance."

Jane giggled at that, but Isabel didn't bother with faking a smile. "With all due respect, Geoffrey, that's not much of an answer."

Blue eyes met hers. "I'm a viscount with an inheritance, my

dear. I don't produce anything. With the exception of heirs, of course."

That couldn't be the truth; if an estate never brought in any income, even the largest inheritance would eventually run out. Taxes, salaries, food, parties, his horse with twelve names – it all cost money. "Investments, then?" she suggested.

"Why so persistent?" he countered. "You've just informed me that your ownership of Nimway Hall is unassailable. I couldn't take it from you even if I wished to do so. Which of course I do not."

"I'm merely curious," she said in her mildest tone, as the footmen brought in a huge platter of roast pig and all the trimmings. "You know much more about Nimway than I know about either Blackbridge or Alton Park."

"All estates are more or less the same, I've found," he drawled. "What holds true for one holds true for most." Geoffrey took another swallow of wine. "It's dull table talk, especially when we've much more interesting things to discuss. Your approving orb and what I hope will be our joined future, for one."

Jane shot to her feet, nearly knocking her chair over backward in her haste. "Oh! Simmons, I need your assistance! You two, as well. At once, if you please!" Grabbing the butler by the arm, she herded him and the two footmen into the drawing room and shut the door behind her.

Isabel's face warmed and her fingers chilled all at the same time. She finished her mouthful of pork. It would hardly suit if she choked to death. "Well, that wasn't at all subtle," she noted.

"No, it wasn't. It was quite convenient, though. I should thank her." Reaching across the corner of the table, he took the fork out of her hand and gripped her fingers. "We do need to talk, after all."

Abruptly she wished she'd asked Adam to join them for dinner. The two men would have spent the meal arguing, of course, but he wouldn't have left the room like the others. Not unless she'd asked him to. And she wouldn't have done so. Something felt...wrong. It felt as though someone were playing a poorly tuned violin in the back of her mind, louder and louder until it downed out everything else.

"...knew it would come to this, from the moment I set eyes on you. Your orb just confirmed what I've known for a fortnight. Be my wife, Isabel. With your resources and my circle of friends, we'll be unstoppable. The envy of all England."

Oh, dear. Oh, dear. "You make it sound very tempting," she hedged, forcing a chuckle.

"It's not a temptation; it's a promise. Say yes. I'll have a special license by week's end."

"A special license? There's no need to rush, surely. My parents are in Florence; it will take at least a month for them to get here after I write them. You must give me a moment to think, Geoffrey. And more time to know you." That sounded both practical and logical – to her ears, at least.

"You're the one with the magic orb to choose your husband," he returned, in the same smooth tone he'd used when he'd spoken about fishing the other day. "It chose me. And you wanted it to be me, didn't you? That's why you asked me here tonight." He curled his fingers around hers. "Say yes."

"I don't—"

The door leading from the hallway shoved open. "Apologies for my tardiness," Adam said, walking in with a laden tray in his arms. "Apparently there was a misunderstanding in the kitchen."

CHAPTER 14

*G*eoffrey let go of her fingers as Adam set the tray down on the table. Wordlessly her steward shifted the plate, utensils, and glass onto the place beside the one Jane had vacated. He sat, sliced off a piece of ham, and stuck it into his mouth.

Adam had interrupted a wedding proposal – *her* wedding proposal. She should be furious. And yet she had to work to keep herself from running over to his chair and hugging him. None of this made any sense. Her thoughts tumbled and swirled like the cyclone she'd argued about with him. More than anything she wanted a minute to think, to breathe, without everyone staring at her.

"You're not wanted here, Driscoll," Geoffrey snapped, his expression for once as flat as his voice.

"I live here, actually," Adam countered.

"Not for long, you don't."

"And I dine with Isabel and Miss Jane every evening," he continued, as if Geoffrey hadn't spoken. "Now be a polite guest and eat your dinner."

Instead the viscount grabbed her hand again, startling her and pulling her further off her literal and figurative balance. "You know he's here because he'll do anything to interfere in my life and happiness. Ignore him. Hell, dismiss him. I'll find you a steward who doesn't have aspirations above his station."

"He's proposed, then?" Adam asked, his voice oddly pitched. "And where will the two of you live? Alton? Blackbridge? Here? London?"

"What the devil does it matter where we'll live?" the viscount cut back in. "It's none of your damned affair."

"Gentlemen, please," Isabel said forcefully. "I haven't agreed to anything, and yes, it does matter where we would live if – if – we married. I'm the guardian of Nimway Hall. This is where I belong."

Alton's fingers tightened around hers. "Then agree now, Isabel. Marry me, and we'll spend enough time at Nimway to satisfy you. Does that assuage your reservations?"

No, it didn't. She left her fingers where they were, beginning to worry that he would pull her out of her chair if she resisted. "It would better assuage my reservations if you would stop viewing this as a decision that needs to be made tonight. There's no reason to hurry so."

"Unless he's already made arrangements to sell off half your cattle or large sections of Balesboro Wood." Adam's expression remained calm despite the coiled, ready sensation she felt from him, and he continued eating.

"The timber rights are mine," Isabel countered, frowning. "They remain mine, whether I marry or not. Why would you say such a thing?"

"He's saying it because it's what he's been planning. Distract you with those beehives you were telling me about and sell off timber lots to the highest bidder. Bits here and there, little enough that you wouldn't notice." Geoffrey narrowed his eyes, pinning Adam with a glare of not just anger, but a hatred that startled her.

"You've thought it all through then, have you?" Adam said.

"That explains why he wants to be rid of me. I'd never allow you to steal from here. To steal from Isabel."

Abruptly Geoffrey released her and lurched to his feet. "This does not concern you," he grated. "I've seen the way you look at her, Driscoll, but look at yourself. You're a farmer in everything but name. You smell of dirt and cattle and horseshit. Even worse, that's all you aspire to. Elizabeth knew that six years ago. She said you liked having dirt beneath your nails. You haven't changed."

Isabel's frown deepened, and something much darker lurched to life in her chest. Who was Elizabeth? Adam's face when she looked over at him had paled to ash. He stood, his own motions smoother and more...deadly than the viscount's. "Say her name again, Alton. I dare you to speak her name again in my presence."

The way he said the words, like an axe cutting through hard wood, struck her with almost physical force. "Who is Elizabeth?" she whispered, odd despair touching her soul. Had there been another woman they'd both loved? Did Adam still love her? He did. She could hear it, feel it, in his voice.

Adam glanced at her, his jaw clenching, before he returned his gaze to the viscount. "You brought it up. Do you wish to explain it, or shall I?"

With a grimace Geoffrey dropped into his chair again. "Considering I've no wish to be attacked for uttering the wrong name, I leave it to you." He jabbed a finger at Adam. "But I did nothing wrong. You chose to make me a monster to assuage your own guilt."

"You—"

"Enough!" Isabel stood, swiping swiftly at her face and hoping neither man noticed her tears. No one's marriage proposal was supposed to tangle into a discussion about another woman. And hers... She'd waited for the orb and her life to all come together, and in none of her imaginings had it ever looked, or felt, like this. "You...punch each other to your heart's content. I'm leaving."

She shoved through the drawing room door, nearly knocking both Jane and Simmons down in the process. So Adam and Geoffrey preferred to fight over a different woman. Fine. She didn't care to be a part of that. Ever.

With Simmons away from the front door, grabbing up a shawl and heading out across the drive was a simple matter. Then she walked. It didn't matter where, as long as she kept moving. The moon was high in the night sky, the air pleasant if a little chilly, and the road in front of her stood out clearly as it curved into the woods.

This was her land, and her well- and frequently traveled road. And if a fox or a badger wanted to argue with her tonight, she felt ready for a fight. The moonlight dimmed as she stepped beneath the leafy canopy, but she could still make out the road and the deer trails that crossed it.

Above her an owl hooted, and the sound echoed once, twice, thrice deeper into Balesboro Wood. It was a lovely, old sound that made her think of ancient times, and lonely enough to suit the hurt in her heart. Adam had said he wanted to woo her. Had he only wanted to do so because he couldn't tolerate the idea of Geoffrey Bell-Spratt winning her favor? It definitely sounded as if they'd fought over this Elizabeth, as well.

Isabel slowed her steps. Simmons had told her that Geoffrey had been engaged, and that the lady in question had died. Had *that* been Elizabeth? Oh, that was even worse. A cherished memory of love that would grow more precious and perfect with time. An image with which she could never hope to compete.

That was her, then, a bone to be fought over by two dogs because the meal they preferred was no longer available. No wonder Adam hadn't wanted to speak of the hostility between him and Alton. She put her hand over her chest and kept walking. It hurt. Her heart physically hurt.

And not because she'd discovered that she was Geoffrey's second choice. After she spoke with him, and as much as she'd wished otherwise, it had been rather apparent that his first love would always be himself. That had become much more evident tonight. But dropping from second to third hadn't troubled her, truthfully. *His* plans hadn't troubled her, except with the growing realization that she didn't wish to be a part of them.

Adam, though... The way he'd reacted at just hearing the name Elizabeth – whoever she was, he'd loved her. Deeply. And that had broken Isabel's heart.

How typical, and how stupid, that she'd realized how important he'd become to her only after she'd made it clear to him that she'd pinned her hopes on Lord Alton. That was irony, wasn't it? To make him her second choice only to discover that she was also his second choice?

But even if she'd belatedly realized that she wanted Adam, the orb seemed to have a different idea. Before she'd become acquainted with Geoffrey, on the surface he'd fulfilled her fairy-tale ideal of a husband – handsome, titled, presumably wealthy, charming, and a believer. Tonight, though, he'd made her uneasy. He'd refused to answer the simplest of questions, turning her queries into a jest and making her seem unreasonable for asking them. Even before Adam had barged in, she'd felt something wrong in the air.

Nothing made any sense. And the one person who might have helped her figure it all out was one of the men from whom she'd fled. And even he couldn't help her reconcile her feelings with what the orb had indicated.

A fallen tree lay across her path, and she stopped. The bower. Isabel's Bower. Had she walked all that way already? It would be a good place to think, and safe from even the most unlikely perils of the road. The brambles scratched her arm and tried to snatch away her shawl, but she managed to duck beneath them and into the clearing.

The three stones glowed a soft white beneath the beams of moonlight, and she could almost hear music on the light breeze. The rustle of leaves and the soft rush of the low waterfall might as well have been ancient voices murmuring words she couldn't decipher.

Isabel ran her hand across the carved surface of the female

stone as she went to stand at the midpoint of the trio. "Is there magic here?" she murmured, lifting her face to the sky. "Are you merely old stones and leaves and water and moonlight, or are you more?"

An owl hooted from one end of the bower, as if to ask who she was to be standing there. And frankly, she couldn't answer the question. The hoot repeated, faded, then repeated on the opposite side of the clearing. A third owl took up the query, then a fourth and a fifth, then so many, so much mournful noise, that she couldn't keep count.

She clapped her hands over her ears. Who was she? The offspring of a sculptor? A half-Italian pretender? Or the daughter of a daughter of a daughter of Somerset, the place where Nimue and Merlin had lived and, legend said, had had a daughter of their own to begin the line from which she claimed descent?

Isabel lowered her hands again. "I am Isabel Jacqueline de Rossi," she stated clearly, refusing to feel self-conscious about declaring herself to a wood full of owls. "I am the daughter of Charlotte Anne Harrington, and the granddaughter of Olivia Heather Devries. And I am the Guardian of Nimway Hall."

The sound died around her. In the space of a half dozen heartbeats the wood became itself again, filled with the rustling of leaves, the chirping of crickets, and the burbling of slow-flowing water. She blinked. Had she just imagined all that? Was she going mad now?

Wood snapped off to her right. Isabel whirled around to look into the gloom, her heart pounding even as she stifled her gasp. Her gaze immediately went to a small circle of light that bobbed and grew larger, ducked, and rose again.

"Isabel?"

For just a second she shut her eyes. *Adam.* "I'm here."

"Thank God." The light lifted and brightened, becoming a lantern as he approached her through the low moss and white flowers. "How the devil did you find your way here on foot and in the dark?"

"I just did," she said, and turned her back on him. "I don't want to talk to you. I'm well. I'll return to the house later."

His quiet footsteps continued toward her. "Alton's demanded a room; he refuses to leave while you're missing, and evidently he asked you a question and insists on receiving an answer." Adam paused. "I assume the question he's referring to is whether you'll marry him," came from much closer behind her.

Her jaw and her fists and her heart clenched, she faced him again. "I assume the same thing, as yes, we both heard him ask me."

Adam's brow dipped in a deep frown. "I hope you're not—"

"This story about the animosity between the two of you," she interrupted. "It was over a woman. Elizabeth. Neither of you liked the outcome, I assume, and now you've found some other chit to fight over. Which makes me, at best, the second choice for you and for him, and at worst, makes me the foolish pawn in your game of one-upmanship."

His face looked ashen in the moonlight, his expression drawing hard and tight as she spoke. "You don't—"

"Considering that," she broke in again, her fury and hurt warming her, "I suppose it doesn't matter which of you I marry. The orb, though, grew warm at his touch, so there you have it."

As she spoke, the disappointment of eighteen years of expecting a fairy-tale life once she reached Nimway, the sadness of having to rethink each thing he'd said to her knowing that he'd likely said them all before and meant them before – it was too much. A tear ran down her cheek and plopped onto the bosom of her gown.

Adam, though, continued to stare at her. She wished he would go away, or at least have the good manners to look away, but he did neither. He just gazed at her, unblinking.

"Nothing to say?" she prompted. "Then I ask you once again to go back to the house. I would like to be alone."

His mouth opened and shut again. "I should have told you everything, after all," he finally said quietly.

"It's too late n—"

"You'll listen to it anyway," Adam snapped, then blew out his breath. "I *did* love Elizabeth, though I'm not convinced Alton ever did. He loved her dowry; I know that."

Isabel couldn't hold back a sob. If he'd told her he'd once had his heart broken, she would have understood. If he'd told her, her own heart wouldn't be breaking now. Turning away again, she put her hands over her ears. "Just go away!"

"Elizabeth... Elizabeth Driscoll. She was my sister, you see," he went on anyway, his voice muffled but still understandable through her palms. "She was a year older than me. Twenty, when Alton met her. He dazzled her, I think, and after two months she accepted his proposal of marriage."

She lowered her hands. The pain in his voice, though – she didn't want to turn around to look at him, for both of their sakes. This... She hadn't expected this. *His sister?*

"Before they were married she went for a ride on her mare, Lily, as she did nearly every morning in the country. This time Lily stepped into a badger hole. She broke both her forelegs, and Elizabeth broke her neck. My father got her back to the house and summoned a doctor and sent for the rest of us, and sent word to Alton."

Adam cleared his throat. "When Alton came to see her, he was the very image of heartbreak, I'm told. My family felt sorry for him, for the life he'd just begun to plan for the two of them that they now would never have. He said he wanted to return with the parson of his own parish, a man who was like a father to him, to sit and pray over her with him. She was becoming feverish but seemed happy to see him, so my father agreed."

"Adam—"

"Let me finish, for God's sake," he hissed. "I never want to tell this story again."

Isabel shut her eyes. "I'm listening."

"I was at my uncle's estate when I received word of all this. Elizabeth and I... We were close. It took me six hours of hard riding to get back home. I ran up to her bedchamber, and found the door shut and her maid, Abby, in the hall, weeping. She said Alton and his parson friend wanted privacy to pray over Elizabeth. I burst in anyway, to find Lizzie so feverish she didn't even recognize me – and this...holy man in the midst of declaring my sister and Alton husband and wife. He wanted her dowry, you see, more than he wanted her. If I hadn't arrived when I did, if I hadn't ripped the marriage license from the priest's hand before Alton could put own signature beside Elizabeth's... And they'd forged her name, because she couldn't move her arms. Or her legs."

Oh, she couldn't stand it any longer. Isabel whirled about to wrap her arms hard around Adam, and his closed around her back. It must have been so awful. So awful. And Alton... To believe she'd thought herself lucky to meet such a handsome, charming, unmarried lord. "You should have told me," she whispered.

"You are so genuinely good," he returned roughly, "if that was what attracted him to you and vice versa, I thought perhaps he'd changed. Become a better man. And I tore up the license and burned it. I had no proof."

As she recalled every conversation she'd ever had with Geoffrey Bell-Spratt, she had to shake her head. "I don't think he's changed. He can't own my timber rights or my water rights, but he could certainly sell off half of Balesboro Wood, especially if we were residing elsewhere." It had always seemed to come back to the timber. Every chat, every jest. And not very subtly, either. She'd just been too trusting to hear it. That money wouldn't have lasted, because once the Wood was gone it would be gone forever, but what a bounty it would have been while it lasted.

Adam held her back from him, and abruptly she worried that she and her jealousy and her...crutch of magic and the orb had ruined this, too. "I want you to know," he said slowly, "that you are the first and only woman with whom I have ever fallen in love. The only woman I ever mean to love."

The keening thrum in her veins, the way her heart galloped –

she couldn't mistake the exultation she felt, or what it meant. "I love you, Adam Driscoll, you impossible man." But the orb! Why in the world had it approved of Lord Alton? And what would happen to her and to Nimway Hall if she went against it?

"Do you have any idea how much I've wanted to hear you say that?" he murmured, brushing his fingers along her cheek and clearly not reading her thoughts.

Another warm tear slid down her face. He was being honest, because he'd always been honest. She needed to be the same. "I do love you," she repeated vehemently, "but the orb chose Alton. I don't know what might happen if I ignore it. I know you think that's ridiculous, but it's important to me. And to Nimway Hall."

His brow furrowed again. "You would still allow that piece of rock and metal to dictate the course of your life?"

"I have to. That's how it's always been."

Releasing her, he dug into his pocket. "Tell me this, then. If your orb chose Alton, why does it keep ending up in my room? I sat down to eat my damned dinner, reached for my glass, and found *it* in my hand instead." He pulled the orb from his coat and held it out to her. "This is why I decided to join you for dinner. For just a second, I thought perhaps something beyond my understanding might be at work."

"It fell off the table in the drawing room," she mused, reaching out to touch the orb. "I don't..."

She trailed off as the moonstone beneath their two sets of fingers began to glow. Softly at first, then more and more brightly it blazed, as bright as sunlight. White touched with iridescent greens and blues and reds buried deep in the stone surrounded the two of them, and reflected off the trio of boulders around them. Far, far away, Isabel could swear she heard a lone female voice, singing a wordless tune.

Adam's green eyes met hers, their emerald startling in its clarity. He held her gaze as the orb's light began slowly to fade, leaving her almost blind in the filtered moonlight and the dim lantern set behind him. "Did you see—"

"I did," he returned, in the same stunned tone. His gaze lowered to the dark moonstone they both still touched. That they'd never touched at the same time until now.

Isabel swallowed. He'd always been so logical. What might this do to him? "Did you hear…"

His eyes snapped up to meet hers again. "A woman. Singing."

Isabel nodded. "Do you believe me now?" she whispered.

"I believe in what I see and hear," he returned. "I saw this. I heard the voice. I heard the owls, as well. They led me here. I have no explanation but the one you've been offering me since you arrived. Magic. Genuine magic."

Putting her hands on either side of his lean face, she leaned up and kissed him. This, *this*, was what finding the love of her life was supposed to feel like. The heat, the lifting sensation, the ecstasy in the rightness of touching him, of being touched by him.

And the explanation for Alton and the orb had to be the simplest one – the viscount had lied. The moonstone hadn't heated when he'd touched it, then instantly cooled the moment she took it back. It had done nothing, just as it had done nothing every time she'd tried to convince it or herself that she was meant to be Lady Alton. Because she wasn't.

Still kissing her, Adam shed his jacket, backing away for a heartbeat to spread it out on the grass. "I'm not waiting any longer," he said, shifting his attention to her jawbone with shiver-inducing kisses and nibbles. "I'm not missing my chance."

"I knew," she breathed, helping him undo the buttons of his dark waistcoat, and that garment joined the first. "I knew it was you, because you kept interrupting every thought I had. But you didn't believe."

"I do now. I believe," he murmured, his tone a heady mix of wonderment and desire. Desire for her. She felt it as well, all the way to her bones – the wish, the need, to be with him, to touch him skin to skin, with nothing separating them. That was why her feet had guided her here tonight. To Isabel's Bower.

Here, with the ancient stone carvings, the moonlight, the

dancing waters of the stream behind them, was where they were meant to be tonight. The small glen felt magical. And this time she didn't need to convince him of that.

"Just tell me no one else is looking for me here," she said, grinning, tangling her fingers into his dark hair, and shivering a little as his big hands slid from her waist to her hips, tugging her closer against him. What had been wrong with her, to ever think for a moment that she'd wanted Alton touching her like this? That had never even occurred to her before now; in her daydreams a match with the viscount had been a companionable partnership. As if he would ever share anything. As if he would ever have cared about her dreams.

"I don't think anyone else knows about this place," he returned, pulling the pins from her hair. Abruptly, though, he stopped, his gaze searching her face. "Isabel, I want you. I want you in my arms, and in my life. You're already in my heart. But I'm selfish enough to want to know that it's not the orb that's convinced you."

"Oh, hang the orb." Pushing aside his hands, she pulled his shirttail from his trousers so she could run her palms up his warm, bare chest. "It took me far too long to figure myself out, but it wasn't the moonstone. I've lived such an unconventional life, and I decided I needed someone...perfect to make me perfect. And because I'm an idiot, I saw exactly what Geoffrey wanted me to see, and I ignored what should have been plain in you."

"You're not an idiot," he countered. "I saw a woman who believed in magic, but not in herself." Adam smiled a little. "I've believed in you nearly from the beginning. And I think tonight you realized you can believe in yourself, as well."

Isabel took a deep breath. She did feel different. After weeks of feeling inadequate and uncertain, tonight she'd made a decision, and she'd done it without the orb. The fact that the moonstone had then confirmed what she already knew in her heart – yes. Everything had changed. And now that she knew for certain what she wanted, nothing was going to get in her way. Not even herself.

"I've had a good teacher," she whispered, helping him lift his shirt off over his head.

He had the body of a man who worked hard, who didn't spend his time at cards or drinking while other men saw to his duties in exchange for coin. More than that, he cared about Nimway Hall, and her, and all of her tenants, and even the bees.

"When I first arrived here," Isabel said slowly, "I imagined the avenue would be lined with knights in shining armor astride white horses, all of them vying to win my hand. And I would solve every problem with a flick of my fingers." She lifted one hand, and he twined his fingers with hers. "The truth I'm discovering is that I'm glad it's not that simple. That nothing is simple or straightforward."

"Are you certain? There is some old armor in the portrait hall, I believe. I might be able to squeeze into it."

A warm shiver ran down her spine, and she chuckled. "No, I think it's too small for you."

His smile heated the rest of her. "I'll take that as a compliment. Now turn around."

She did so, and as his fingers opened the quartet of buttons at the nape of her neck she shivered again, every inch of her awake and anticipating his touch. A forefinger trailed down her spine, his warm mouth following. *Goodness.* Most of her daydreams became rather nebulous at this point, but this was no daydream, no fairytale. And she was exceedingly thankful for that.

He moved around to face her, his gaze on her face as he bent down to gather the mauve-and-black material of her skirt in his hands, then slowly drew it up above her knees, past her thighs, her hips, and upward. "Arms up," he murmured, another slight, sensuous smile touching his mouth.

When Isabel complied, Adam pulled her gown and shift over her head, then dropped them to the ground as if they'd ceased to matter. She watched as his gaze lowered, watched as he took her in from her feet to her face. Her skin warmed, not with embarrassment, but with a heated anticipation. The orb could fly up into the air and strike the moon and she wouldn't have spared it a glance. Just as well, then, that the claw-gripped moonstone seemed to approve.

"You belong here in Isabel's Bower," he said, "with the moonlight touching your skin. A forest nymph, too lovely to be real."

"I see you've come to embrace the idea of magic fairly quickly," she returned, lifting an eyebrow.

Adam laughed. "I surrender. You *are* magic. I believe in you, so I must believe in magic." Keeping his gaze on her face, he kicked out of his boots, unfastened his trousers, and stepped out of them.

Oh, my. While she'd seen a plenitude of naked men carved in marble and plaster back in Florence, none of those statues did Adam Driscoll justice. He was…magnificent. And aroused, with wanting her. She knew that already, but now she saw the evidence of it.

When he took that one step back to her, she wasn't certain what to expect. It certainly wasn't that he would sweep her into his arms, and she gasped and wrapped her own arms around his neck. He kissed her again, deliriously long and deep, then knelt on the edge of his coat and set her down gently in front of him.

She refused to relinquish her grip on him, and he settled along her body as she sank onto her back. She was finished with making mistakes – or at least ones of the magnitude of the one she'd nearly made by not truly *seeing* the man who'd stood at her shoulder almost from the moment she'd arrived in Somerset. Then he slid down and took one of her breasts in his mouth, and her mind stopped thinking at all. There was far too much to feel.

He licked and teased at her breasts until she couldn't breathe. Just when she felt ready to faint he lifted his head and moved up to kiss her again. That seemed to only be a distraction, though, because while his mouth was occupied, his fingers trailed up the insides of her thighs, then touched her…there.

Isabel jumped, then uttered a groan she couldn't stifle as he slid a finger inside her. Heat spread from her center out to the tips of her fingers and her toes, sending a delicious shudder down her spine. Beneath his ministrations, even as she writhed in pleasure, she felt...everything. A part of everything. Him, the land, the night, the trees around them – together they became whole.

"I'm hearing music again," he murmured, as he nibbled at her earlobe. "Is this going to happen every time I'm with you? Because I intend to have you very frequently."

Her eyes practically rolled back in her head. She could hear it too, more as a rhythm matching her fast pulse than with her ears. "I hear it as well, and I have no idea," she returned, her voice sounding ragged even to her own ears. "I look forward to finding out."

As she spoke she reached between them to brush her fingers against his hard manhood, and had the satisfaction of seeing him jump. God. Because while this might be about her becoming a woman and the Guardian of Nimway Hall, it was at least as much about the two of them, together.

"Show me what's next," she breathed, arching her back as a second finger joined his first.

"This isn't enough?" he asked with a grin, lifting his head to look down at her.

"I feel very...ah, wonderful," she managed, "but you seem to be in an unsatisfied state." She wrapped her fingers around his shaft.

Adam drew in a hard breath. "Pleasing you pleases me," he returned, his own tone not quite steady. "But you have asked me to teach you some things."

"Then teach me this."

Moving up the length of her again, trailing kisses along her skin as he rose, Adam nudged her knees apart. *Alive.* Every inch of her felt so alive. And that was because of him. "I'm told this may hurt," he said, gazing at her intently. "I know of no other way to make you mine, and it won't hurt again. But I still need to know you're ready. That this – me – is what you want."

He would stop if she asked, because he was a gentleman, a true gentleman, down to his bones. But then she would never know what came next, for her or for the two of them. And she very much wanted to know. Isabel raised her head and kissed him. "I'm ready."

Settling himself between her legs, Adam caught her mouth again, at the same time canting his hips forward. With an exquisite filling sensation he entered her. Deep inside her she felt pressure, then a sharp pain that made her wince, before he sank deeply into her. Isabel squeezed her eyes shut, determined not to cry out. A few hard beats of her heart passed before she realized how very still Adam held himself inside her.

Opening her eyes again, she forced a weak laugh, the feeling of him buried inside her intensifying as she took a deep breath. "I won't break," she said unsteadily.

"Good," he whispered back, his voice hard and husky. "You're Nimway's guardian, but Nimway had best understand that you and I are a pair. Forever."

With another deep, openmouthed kiss he began moving inside her. Arching her back, Isabel dug her fingers into his back, holding on as he rocked into her. *Good heavens.* Her legs fell open with an abandon she would never have expected of herself, but all that mattered was her being as close to him as she could get.

He moved slowly, then faster and faster, tension growing tighter and tighter inside her. She moaned, wrapping her ankles around his thighs to invite him in even more deeply. Abruptly everything went white, and she shattered into a thousand pulsing, shivering pieces.

Above her Adam groaned, entering her slowly and deeply, carrying her farther into ecstasy. As sound and sight began to return he sped his pace again, faster and harder until with a deep growl he climaxed, spilling his seed inside her.

Both of them breathing hard, he lowered his head against her shoulder, then rolled the two of them so that he lay beneath her. Under her cheek his heart beat strong and fast, matching her own. And this, this connection between them, this was perfection. She never wanted to move again, never wanted to leave the warm circle of his arms. "I love you, Adam."

"I love you, Isabel," he returned without hesitation, his low voice resonating through her. "And now tell me, in front of the orb and the stone carvings and the owls and the forest and Nimway Hall, will you marry me?"

He would make her a better Guardian. He already had. And more than that, he would be her partner, her equal, and her love. And that was what Nimway Hall was. Love. "Yes, beneath the moon and all the stars, I will marry you. Very happily."

As he kissed her again, very softly and gently, she could feel his smile against her mouth, matching hers. "I've been trying to find an explanation for why, when I first arrived here and despite everything going wrong, it felt like...home. Now I realize it's because this place, and I, were both waiting for you."

That was quite possibly the best compliment she'd ever received, "I'm just glad you and the orb and the house were patient enough to give me time to figure myself out." Everything had tried to tell her, she realized. Thank goodness she'd opened her eyes and her heart enough to listen and to understand.

And now she – they – had one more thing to see to. Nimway had an unwanted guest who'd badly overstayed his welcome, and before she could declare everything perfect, he needed to go. At once.

CHAPTER 15

*G*eoffrey Bell-Spratt paced. She'd been gone for better than two hours. If Isabel had fallen off the escarpment or drowned in the lake or something equally final, the property would revert to her mother or grandmother. That was the oddness of a female-owned property not controlled by the rules of inheritance. And it would never do. She needed to be alive and well. His reputation wouldn't withstand being accused of a deathbed marriage twice.

Cursing under his breath, he left the room he'd taken for himself and strode down the hallway and the main stairs. The wretched, stiff-backed butler still stood in the foyer like a dour gargoyle. "Any word?" he asked.

"I would not keep such information to myself, my lord," Simmons said, not moving. "Of that, you may be certain."

"Then have my horse saddled, and I'll lend a hand in searching for Isabel."

"You don't know the land, my lord. One wrong turn and you'll be vanished, as well, and then we'd have to go find you. And it's never wise for a stranger to be wandering Balesboro Wood in the dark, anyway. Or in the daylight, for that matter."

He could protest that he'd been poring over maps and therefore knew the property's trails as well as any man could, but for the moment he preferred to keep that information to himself. It would never do for someone to think he'd overstepped. Not before his position here was officially secured. "I will only be patient for so long," he returned. "Your mistress and I are to be married, you know. Her presence is required in order for that to happen." He started to turn away, then paused. "And I'm worried for her safety, of course."

Yes, one did need to show concern. It looked well, and he was quite proficient at it, if he said so himself.

"Duly noted, my lord. Now if you would be so kind as to return upstairs, the household won't have to fret over where to find you."

Geoffrey made his own note, that once he and Isabel were wed, the butler would be replaced by someone less high in the instep. Several things here would change, and several men would be let go – the butler being second on his list. His first target was hopefully out falling off the escarpment and saving them all the bother of having to send him away.

He ascended the staircase again. The bannisters were in good condition, a well-carved and expensive mahogany. He'd also noted the fine carved-marble fireplace in the dining room. The half-naked female bore a passing resemblance to Isabel, though that might have been his imagination.

After marriage the house would not become his, but once he removed Isabel to Alton Park there would be a great deal he could do to earn a bit here and there. Moving out furniture in unused rooms under the pretense of renovations, shipping items off for "repairs" only to discover they'd been ruined in the attempt – providing Isabel de Rossi returned safe and sound tonight, there would be ample opportunity to unofficially render what some antiquated papers declared to be hers, his. As it traditionally would and should have been.

Rather than return to the bedchamber he'd made a show of

claiming before the bony-faced butler could arrange to put him on his horse and shoo him away – which had apparently been successful since the man now refused to let him out the front door – Geoffrey continued down the quiet hallway to take stock of some of the other rooms. It was rather like going shopping, looking at furniture and knick-knacks and deciding which ones could be disposed of with no one noting.

One room looked as though it had been set up as a makeshift office, with floor plans and room drawings cluttering a table. Hmm. That could be useful. Selecting one of the plans which detailed the layout of the entire house, he folded it up and slipped it into his coat pocket.

"Who are you, sir, and what are you doing here?"

Stifling a surprised curse, Geoffrey whipped around to see a short, bespectacled man with graying red hair and a slightly ill-fitting jacket that screamed secondhand. The distinct odor of mildew touched his nose as the fellow moved closer. "I am Lord Alton," he proclaimed grandly. "Who are you?"

"Hodgins. The architect."

"Ah. What are you designing, Hodgins the architect?"

"An orangery." The little fellow frowned. "Are you lost, my lord? Nimway Hall is rather…sprawling."

With one of his famous charming smiles, Geoffrey shook his head. "Were you not informed? Miss Isabel has gone missing. I'm helping search for her."

"Oh, dear! Let me put my things down, and I'll join you."

Damnation. He did not wish to be accompanied by the odor of mildew, or by a common architect. "We'll cover more area if you take the attic rooms," Geoffrey said, thinking quickly.

"Of course. Right away."

Once the small fellow hurried off, Geoffrey made his way down the opposite wing. The house was clearly very old, despite its careful upkeep. That was good; old, well-cared-for things brought more money. He fingered a vase on a hallway table, making a note of its location for later.

The next room he entered was obviously Driscoll's, and he swiftly returned to the hallway. No sense wasting time in there. Yes, the steward would definitely have to go, but that shouldn't be too difficult to arrange. Isabel had a very soft heart. A tale about how Driscoll had kept him from marrying Elizabeth when that had been the chit's dying wish or some such thing – that should suffice.

At the end of the hallway the double doors would be the master bedchamber. If Isabel kept black candles or tarot cards there, that would give him a way to find an additional motivation for her to marry him, if his charm alone proved to be insufficient. People who claimed to have magic or be witches could well find themselves stripped of their property and removed to Bedlam.

The lamp outside the doors flickered and went out. He didn't feel a breeze, but all old houses were drafty. Extra candles sat about rooms for just that reason. He freed one from the small drawer in the hall table and turned back up the hallway for the previous lamp.

As he reached the wall sconce, that flame also wavered and went out. In response, a slight shiver of uneasiness went through him. Geoffrey rolled his shoulders. It was all nonsense and shoddy upkeep. The master bedchamber would have a fire in the hearth, and that would give him enough light to find any cat bones or mandrake root or any other items of magic she'd hopefully collected. Turning around again, he headed back down the hallway.

One of the doors opened as he reached out his hand toward it. First it bumped a few inches, then it swung wide open. Geoffrey stopped in his tracks. "This is ridiculous," he muttered, swallowing. "Do you expect me to believe any of this? Parlor tricks, at best."

Silence answered him. That was because nothing was there, he decided. The same drafts that had extinguished the lights had simply pushed open a poorly secured door. And a breeze was not going to make him turn tail. Not when a prize lay right at his fingertips. His only regret now was that he hadn't brought a tarot card or two with him.

He stepped forward again, only to stop as a shadow crossed in front of the doorway. Two glowing green eyes appeared in the dim depths of the room beyond, the height of a man but clearly not human. For several moments the eyes gazed at him, through him, unblinking.

The cat, he remembered abruptly, and his heart began beating again. The stray cat Isabel had found. It must be atop a wardrobe, he decided, giving the illusion that the long-tailed rat was taller and larger than it actually was.

"Shoo, cat," he ordered, and entered the room.

The fire in the hearth had burned down to embers, a sure sign that the room's mistress was late returning. Geoffrey squatted down to stir the fire and add another log. When he straightened and turned around, his heart skittered again. No cat lay atop a wardrobe...and no wardrobe stood where he'd seen the eyes.

That spot was bare wall, framed by a pair of pastoral land-scapes depicting Glastonbury Abbey and the stone henge. "What the devil?" he whispered, instantly regretting his choice of words. With a frown he squared his shoulders and approached the wall. The paint was smooth, with no sign of the scratches or claw marks that would have been necessary for a cat to climb the wall.

It made no sense. And he didn't particularly want to remain in the room any longer. On the other hand, finding a bit more evidence that Isabel either believed in or dabbled in magic could provide him with any leverage he might need. Given a choice between him and Bedlam, even a stubborn chit like Isabel should have no trouble deciding.

He opened the nightstand drawer. A sleek gray shape launched at him, hissing, from behind the floor-length curtains. At the same moment the fire behind him roared with heat and light, an instant inferno. Geoffrey yelped, scrambling backward until he tripped over the corner of the bed and fell on his backside.

"What are you doing in here?" Isabel's voice demanded.

Geoffrey started to roll onto his hands and knees, but the cat leaped onto his head, claws and teeth digging into his scalp. He shrieked, batting at the thing.

For a half dozen stunned heartbeats Isabel watched Geoffrey Bell-Spratt roll about on her floor, a small gray cat attached to his head. Beside her Adam shifted, but she put a hand on his arm. "He doesn't precisely look menacing," she whispered.

"He looks like a lunatic," Adam returned, his voice much louder. "A description I'll happily pass on at the first opportunity. Get off the damned floor, Alton."

"Mist! Get away from him!" Isabel seconded, her concern more for the little cat's safety than for the viscount's.

With a last hiss and spit the cat ran off down the hallway, escaping between her and Adam's legs.

"The kitten's gone, Alton," Adam stated, reaching out to twine his fingers with hers. "Get up before I assist you with my boot."

The viscount staggered to his feet. "This is the devil's house!" he rasped, blood trickling down his face.

To the right side of the room the very-bright fire in the hearth popped and began to dim. Alton had evidently been attempting to burn down the house. She opened her mouth to tell him to remove himself at once, but he flinched away from the fire and made a distinct whimpering sound.

"If this was the devil's house," she said, "you would be much more welcome than you presently are. What are you doing in my bedchamber?"

"T-This..." he stammered, waving his scratched hand about the room, "this is real! All the idiotic orbs and rainbows and all the other simpering nonsense you kept prattling on about. It's real. I thought..." He paused again, uttering a choked laugh edged with hysteria. "I thought you were a moronic, pretty lunatic. I thought if you had a wish to stay out of Bedlam you w—"

"Ah," Adam interrupted, his voice dropping into a growl.

"While I don't mind hearing all the offal spewing out of your mouth, you've insulted Isabel."

"She—"

"If she decided, wisely, that she didn't want to marry you, you meant to threaten her with exposing her belief in magic, didn't you?" Adam interrupted again. "Caught between you and a residence in Bedlam, she'd have no choice but to give you control of all the timber on her property."

That was all it had been, she realized as Adam spoke. Geoffrey hadn't believed her, either. The difference was that Adam had argued, while the viscount had encouraged her to speak what he considered to be nonsense in order to use her beliefs against her later.

"Geoffrey," she said, releasing Adam's hand and stalking up to her would-be beau, "I will not be marrying you. I'm marrying Adam. And if you show your face on Nimway property ever again, I will turn you into a toad. A very fat, very ugly toad. Do you understand?"

He barked another half-hysterical laugh. "A toad."

After what Adam had told her, even a toad was better than he deserved. "Yes. A toad. Do you understand?" she repeated.

His light-blue eyes focused on her. "A toad. Yes, I understand. Don't worry. I have no reason to ever come anywhere near here ever again." He touched his head, then looked at the blood on his fingers. "Giant green-eyed devil men, devil cats, hellfire – it's all yours, Driscoll. Now get out of my way."

Thankfully, Adam stepped aside to allow Alton to pass. A moment later she heard him bellowing for his horse. Adam had ordered Staffordshire in the Morning Light saddled the moment they'd returned to the house, so she imagined that within a very few minutes and beneath the watchful eyes of Simmons and the grooms, Geoffrey Bell-Spratt would be well on his way back to Blackbridge. And good riddance.

"Giant green-eyed men?" Adam repeated, moving up behind her. "Is there something you haven't told me?"

She faced him. "I have no idea what he was talking about," she said, lifting a hand to cup his cheek. "You've never lied to me, have you?"

He frowned. "Of course not."

"I know. And Geoffrey did nothing *but* lie."

Adam slid his hands around her waist. "He wanted what you have. I want *you*."

Isabel smiled, leaning up along his chest to kiss him and relishing in the warm intimacy between them. He'd been a friend long before she'd realized it, and she'd begun to trust and admire him almost despite herself. But now... Now he was everything. He and Geoffrey both believed in the magic of this place now, but only Adam had seen the wonder of it. Because, she realized, he trusted her as much as she trusted him.

"Oh. Oh!" Jane exclaimed from the doorway, her hands flying to her mouth. "I saw Lord Alton go fleeing out the door and I thought, 'Good heavens', but now here I am and you're – well, Mr. Driscoll is in your bedchamber, and—"

"I invited Lord Alton to leave," Isabel said, remaining in the circle of Adam's arms. "Mr. Driscoll and I are getting married."

Jane clapped her hands together. "Thank goodness. I have to say, Lord Alton was pretty, but I'm not entirely certain he meant everything he said."

"I wish you'd shared that with me, Jane."

"It doesn't matter now," Adam cut in. "Everything's as it should be. In the morning I'll write my parents, and I assume you'll wish to do the same for yours and your grandparents."

Isabel nodded. She wanted everything to begin at once, and she had to remind herself that everything *was* as it should be. There was no reason to hurry. Not here.

Glancing up at Adam, she pulled away from him and returned to the door. "We'll see you in the morning, Jane," she said crisply.

"I – What? Good hea—"

"Good night," Isabel said firmly, and closed the door on her companion's surprised face.

When she turned around, the sight of Adam's amused expression warmed her to her bones. "That was rather bold," he commented. "The entire household will know you're a ruined woman within the next five minutes."

"And yet I simply don't care," she replied with a grin, returning to him. She dug into his coat pocket for the orb. When she lifted it, it busily did its usual nothing. "Touch it with me," she said.

The moment his fingers touched the moonstone next to hers, it began its soft glow, lighting and warming the room. As she considered it, it made sense that only the two of them together made the magic work. Adam was her equal, her partner, her love.

When she woke in the morning, close in his arms, she looked toward the table where they'd put the orb. It was gone, Mist curled up asleep in its spot – though how the cat had gotten through the closed door, she had no idea.

This time she didn't think the orb would be reappearing elsewhere. It had shown her – and shown Adam – what they needed to see. The moonstone wasn't needed any longer. Nor would it be, until their own daughter was ready to become the Guardian of Nimway Hall.

Fingers stroked the back of her left shoulder. "Did you know you have a birthmark here?" Adam murmured in a low voice. "And unless I'm seeing things, it greatly resembles the orb."

She turned over to face him. "Yes. As far as I know, every one of Nimway's guardians bears the same mark. I nearly showed it to you a week ago, but I didn't care to be ruined for no good reason."

"Remarkable," he said, touching her cheek. "Magic all around me, and I refused to see it until last night."

Isabel kissed him, brushing hair from his forehead. "And I nearly refused to see you until it was too late. But now that you know magic is real, come to the window with me."

She rose, naked, and he slid from beneath the blankets to pad after her, wrapping his arms around her as she pulled open the curtains and leaned back against his hard chest.

"What is it?" he asked.

"I want you to see the sunrise."

"I have seen a sunrise or two before," he murmured, kissing the top of her head.

"Not like this, you haven't."

THE END

DISCOVER MORE IN THE NIMWAY HALL SERIES

1750 - Jacqueline by Stephanie Laurens
1794 - Charlotte by Karen Hawkins
1940 - Josie by Linda Needham

DISCOVER MORE BY SUZANNE ENOCH

Traditional Regencies

The Black Duke's Prize
Angel's Devil

Regency Historicals
Lady Rogue
Stolen Kisses

The Bancroft Brothers
By Love Undone
Taming Rafe

With This Ring
Reforming a Rake
Meet Me at Midnight
A Matter of Scandal

DISCOVER MORE BY SUZANNE ENOCH

Traditional Regencies Continued...

Lessons in Love
The Rake
London's Perfect Scoundrel
England's Perfect Hero

Anthologies

One True Love (from The Further Observations of Lady Whistledown)

A Touch of Scandal (from Lady Whistledown Strikes Back)

The Griffin Family
Sin and Sensibility
An Invitation to Sin
Something Sinful
Sins of a Duke

DISCOVER MORE BY SUZANNE ENOCH

The Notorious Gentlemen
After The Kiss
Before the Scandal
Always a Scoundrel

The Adventurers' Club
The Care and Taming of a Rogue
A Lady's Guide to Improper Behavior
Rules of an Engagement

The Scandalous Brides
A Beginner's Guide to Rakes
Taming an Impossible Rogue
Rules to Catch a Devilish Duke
The Handbook to Handling His Lordship

Standalone Short Stories
Good Earl Hunting

DISCOVER MORE BY SUZANNE ENOCH

The Scandalous Highlanders
One Hot Scot (a short story)
The Devil Wears Kilts
Rogue with a Brogue
Mad, Bad and Dangerous in Plaid
Some Like it Scot

No Ordinary Hero
Hero in the Highlands
My One True Highlander
A Devil in Scotland

DISCOVER MORE BY SUZANNE ENOCH

Contemporary Romantic Suspense

Flirting with Danger
Don't Look Down
Billionaires Prefer Blondes

Twice the Temptation (half historical, half contemporary)
A Touch of Minx

ABOUT THE AUTHOR

A lifelong lover of books, Suzanne Enoch has been writing them since she learned to read. She is the author of two well-received traditional Regencies, 24 and counting England-set Historical Romances, four contemporary Romantic Suspense novels, and a growing number of Scottish Highlands Historical Romances including the October 2016 release of HERO IN THE HIGHLANDS (Book One in the No Ordinary Hero trilogy).

A native and current resident of Southern California, Suzanne lives with a green parakeet named Kermit, some very chirpy finches, and a small army of Star Wars figures (including a life-size Yoda). Her books regularly appear on the *New York Times* and *USA Today* bestseller lists, and when she's not busily working on her next book or staging fights with action figures, she likes to read, play video games, and go to the movies with her large and supportive village.

CPSIA information can be obtained
at www.ICGtesting.com
Printed in the USA
LVHW03s1340090718
583149LV00005B/684/P